*His gaze softened, and, reaching out,
Jed traced the line of her jaw.*

His touch left a trail of fire. Startled by the intensity of her reaction, she looked up into his eyes. Her anger vanished as her breath locked in her lungs, and the urge to reach out and test the feel of his jawline was so strong, her hand began to move upward.

A flicker of surprise showed in his eyes. "Emily?" He said her name in a slow, questioning drawl.

You're making a fool of yourself! her inner voice screamed at her. She jerked her gaze away from his and took a step back out of his reach.

His eyes narrowed with purpose. Moving toward her, he caught her chin and forced her to look up at him.

But she'd spent a great deal of time since the accident promising herself that no man was going to make a fool of her again. "Don't," she ordered warningly, again jerking free from his touch.

Dear Reader,

Welcome to Silhouette Romance—experience the magic of the wonderful world where two people fall in love. Meet heroines who will make you cheer for their happiness, and heroes (be they the boy next door or a handsome, mysterious stranger) who will win your heart. Silhouette Romance reflects the magic of love—sweeping you away with books that will make you laugh and cry; heartwarming, poignant stories that will move you time and time again.

In the next few months, we're publishing romances by many of your all-time favorites such as Diana Palmer, Brittany Young, Annette Broadrick and many others. Your response to these authors and others in Silhouette Romance has served as a touchstone for us, and we're pleased to bring you more books with Silhouette's distinctive medley of charm, wit and—above all—*romance*.

During 1991, we have many special events planned. Don't miss our WRITTEN IN THE STARS series. Each month in 1991, we're proud to present you with a book that focuses on the hero—and his astrological sign.

I hope you'll enjoy this book and all of the stories to come. Come home to romance—Silhouette Romance—for always!

Sincerely,

Tara Gavin
Senior Editor

ELIZABETH AUGUST

Ready-Made Family

Silhouette Romance

Published by Silhouette Books New York

America's Publisher of Contemporary Romance

SILHOUETTE BOOKS
300 E. 42nd St., New York, N.Y. 10017

READY-MADE FAMILY

ISBN: 0-373-08771-3

First Silhouette Books printing January 1991

Printed in the U.S.A.

Books by Elizabeth August

Silhouette Romance

Author's Choice #554
Truck Driving Woman #590
Wild Horse Canyon #626
Something So Right #668
The Nesting Instinct #719
Joey's Father #749
Ready-Made Family #771

ELIZABETH AUGUST

lives in Wilmington, Delaware, with her husband, Doug, and her three boys, Douglas, Benjamin and Matthew. She began writing romances soon after Matthew was born. She'd always wanted to write.

Elizabeth does counted-cross stitching to keep from eating at night. It doesn't always work. "I love to bowl, but I'm not very good. I keep my team's handicap high. I like hiking in the Shenandoahs as long as we start up the mountain so that the return trip is down rather than vice-versa." She loves to go to Cape Hatteras to watch the sun rise over the ocean.

Elizabeth August has also published books under the pseudonym Betsy Page.

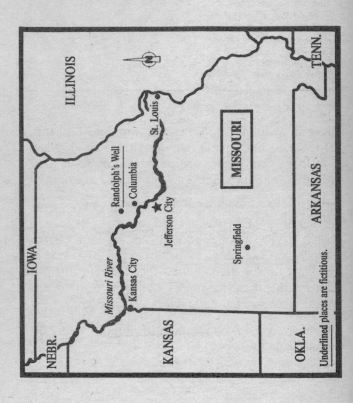

Chapter One

Thelma O'Riley had the look of a woman ready to do battle. "Those children need someone who is dependable!"

Jed Sawyer stood frowning down at his housekeeper. Thelma was fifty-seven. Even drawn up to her full height as she was now, her plumpish five-foot-two-inch body was small compared to his muscular six foot-one-inch frame. But the copper-red hair that was still discernable among the gray gave warning that this lady was not easily reckoned with when she set her mind to something.

"You need to find someone more mature, someone more reliable," Thelma continued. "Someone who understands responsibility."

Jed raked a hand through his sweat-soaked hair. It was getting near planting time and he'd spent nine hours on a tractor today turning soil only to come back to the house to discover that his latest live-in baby-sitter had packed and gone that afternoon. She'd left a note explaining that she and her boyfriend had made up and he didn't like her living under another man's roof. She'd also been honest enough to add that she hadn't thought looking after four children could be so strenuous.

He was tired and hungry and in no mood to deal with this latest problem.

"There aren't any locals left," he muttered, mentally ticking off the names of the four women who had come on a trial basis. Two he had dismissed because he felt they were too insensitive. The third had quit when her daughter had suddenly announced she was getting a divorce and needed her mother to baby-sit her children while she went out and found a job. Now Nora was gone. He'd been certain she would work out. She was young, full of energy, and the kids had liked her.

"Nora wasn't right for the job, anyway," Thelma said as if reading his mind. "She wasn't mature enough. Those kids need a loving, but firm hand. They need someone with a mother's touch. Losing their parents has been a shock to them."

"This whole business has been a shock to me," Jed muttered, glancing toward the closed kitchen door. He knew that beyond it and down the hall, his brother's four children would be in the den watching television. The two boys resembled their father. They were sturdily built with complexions that tanned easily and roundish, fun-loving faces. They even had the same color brown eyes and hair. The girls were miniatures of their mother, with pretty, delicate-featured faces and blond hair and blue eyes. Drew, who was nine and the oldest, and Dennis, who was five, would be sitting Indian-style on the floor. The two girls would be on the couch. Linda, who at a mere seven years old was desperately trying to act like the mother of the group, would be sitting with her arm wrapped protectively around Amy, who was three. In his mind's eye he could see Amy staring up at him, her big blue eyes reminding him of a lost and bewildered kitten. All the children had been strongly affected by their parents' deaths, and he was trying to help them. But instant fatherhood had not been easy.

"What you need is a wife," Thelma finished sternly. "You're thirty. It's time you settled down."

Jed scowled at her. "I can't even find someone who's willing to stick around and take care of my nieces and nephews for money. What makes you think any woman would want to marry me and take on this passel of kids?"

"I admit you've got a point," she conceded. "It's a sure bet that none of the women you usually date would fit the bill." Her stance became even more rigid. "However, something has to be done. I hate to threaten you. You're like a son to me, but I've raised five children of my own and I'm too old to start again. Either you get someone permanent or I'll be the next to leave."

Jed studied her in a stony silence. He was fairly certain she was lying. She'd been the housekeeper here for the past fifteen years, ever since her husband had died. She had a good heart and he didn't think she would desert him now. But he knew she was right. Taking care of the kids was too much for her. "I'll call an employment agency tomorrow," he promised. "I'll find a governess...nanny...whatever...but it will be someone who will stay."

The frown on Thelma's face deepened. "I don't like the idea of a stranger moving in." She cleared her throat. "There is one person you haven't considered who might be perfect for the job."

Jed's gaze narrowed. Now he was going to find out why his housekeeper had made that threat. Obviously whoever she had in mind was someone she didn't expect him to accept easily. "And who would that be?"

Placing both hands on her hips, Thelma faced him levelly. "Emily Hartley."

"Emily?" Jed stared at her as if he thought having four children around the house had put too great a strain on Thelma's sanity.

But Thelma didn't waver. "Yes," she said. "I know she's been a bit difficult to get along with these past four years, but she's got good reason. I've known her all her life and I remember her before that drunk in the truck crashed into her father's car. She was a kind good-hearted girl and down deep inside her I know that's how she still is. She used to always help in the church nursery. She's a natural with children. She would have been a wonderful mother if that accident hadn't put an end to any hopes of motherhood for her."

Jed couldn't deny that Emily had good reason for being the way she was. The accident that had injured her so severely had also claimed her parents. But that had not been the end of losses for Emily. "She'd never help me out. She considers men to be the scum of the earth," he pointed out curtly.

Thelma scowled. "After the way that Howard Parker treated her, she should. The man should have been horsewhipped." The scowl turned to a determined line. "But what's past is past. It's time for Emily to get over it and those kids need someone dependable to help raise them."

"They do need someone dependable," he agreed. "But I don't think Emily Hartley is the answer." Drawing a tired breath, he added in a tone that indicated he didn't want to discuss this any further at the moment, "I'll find someone, but right now I need a shower and some dinner." Turning, he strode out of the kitchen.

Emily Hartley. That was absurd. He couldn't believe Thelma had even suggested the woman. Emily had always been a serious-minded female, but now there was a grimness about her that warned people, especially men, to keep their distance. He wanted someone warm and loving for the children.

As he started up the stairs, Linda came out of the den. "Is Nora coming back?" she asked, an edge of defensiveness in her young voice.

"No. I told you already that she's not," Drew answered for Jed, following his sister into the hall. "Nobody wants to stay with us."

Linda's jaw trembled, then stiffened. "You'll always stay with us, won't you, Uncle Jed?"

Kneeling in front of the two children, Jed drew them into his arms. "I'll always be here for you," he assured them gruffly.

Later, as he stood with the hot shower pouring down over his tired body, he had to admit that Thelma was right about one thing—the children needed real stability in their lives.

But Emily Hartley? He shook his head. He still couldn't understand why Thelma had suggested her. His housekeeper was normally a very sound thinker.

Closing his eyes, he stood so that the water cascaded over his head and face. Suddenly an almost forgotten image filled his mind. It was a Sunday afternoon in summer, several years ago. The congregation of the church both he and Emily attended was having a potluck dinner following the service. Some of the boys had been playing on the swings, and the Miller boy had decided to jump off his swing when it was in midair. He'd landed badly and broken his leg. It had been a bad break; the bone had splintered and come through the skin. It had been Emily who had come to the child's rescue. She'd been compassionate and calm. Jed had driven her, the boy and the boy's parents to the hospital. During the ride it had been Emily who had soothed the child and kept his mother from becoming hysterical. At the hospital he and Emily had stayed, giving the parents support while the doctors worked to set the leg. Through those long hours, she had been such a pillar of support he had begun to think that maybe she was simply cold, and seeing the boy injured hadn't affected her that much.

But afterward, when he'd driven her home, he'd glanced toward her and been surprised to see a thin trail of tears roll down her cheek.

"Are you all right?" he asked, pulling off the road and parking on the shoulder.

"I was so scared for him," she confessed shakily.

She looked so vulnerable, Jed found himself tempted to draw her into his arms. But he'd never been really certain how to treat Emily. She'd always kept her distance from him. So, instead, he settled for brushing the thin stream of water from her cheek with his thumb. He'd been surprised by how soft and warm her skin had felt to his touch. "You were real good with the boy and his mother," he'd said encouragingly, hoping she wouldn't break down and start sobbing. Crying women always unnerved him.

"Thanks." She suddenly flushed with embarrassment as if just then realizing she'd been crying. Straightening her shoulders, she brushed away the last vestiges of wetness. "I don't usually dissolve into tears." She forced a small smile. "You were real good yourself." Then giving a nod in the direction of the road, she added, "I really should be getting home."

In spite of her attempt to look calm and once again in control, he noticed that her hand shook slightly when she raised it to brush a strand of hair from where it had stuck to her still-damp cheek. Again he had the most tremendous urge to draw her into his arms and comfort her. But instead he simply said, "Yeah, me too," and restarted the engine.

For the next couple of weeks, she crossed his mind a great deal. She had proven to be much gentler than he had thought. And he couldn't deny he'd liked the feel of her skin. But she was engaged to Howard Parker. Besides, she wasn't really his type. He preferred women who took life a little less seriously.

It was a little after two in the morning when Jed was awakened by a child's cries. He dragged himself out of bed, pulled on a pair of jeans and made his way down the hall to the girls' room. Drew and Dennis were already there.

"Hush," Drew was admonishing Amy in a worried whisper. "Uncle Jed needs his sleep."

Linda was standing beside Amy's bed gently caressing Amy's tearstained cheek while Dennis stood beside her looking uncertain as to what to do.

"I want my mommy," Amy was sobbing.

"What's wrong?" Jed asked, entering the room and walking toward the bed.

"Amy just had a nightmare," Drew explained. "We're sorry she woke you up. We'll take care of it."

The boy looked so anxious it tore at Jed's heart. Did Drew think his uncle would throw them all out because they disturbed his rest? "It's all right," he assured them. "We're family here. We're supposed to help one another." Approaching the bed, he lifted Amy into his arms.

"I want my mommy," she sobbed again, a fresh flood of tears streaming down her cheeks.

Jed wasn't certain what to do. The child needed a woman's touch. But he was all that was available. Grabbing up a blanket, he wrapped it around her and then carried her to the rocking chair. "You can all go back to bed," he said gently. "I'll sit and rock Amy for a while."

"We don't want to be a bother," Drew insisted. "I can rock her."

"I really don't mind," Jed assured him once again.

"It's time the rest of you were asleep." Thelma stopped any further protest by Drew as she entered the room. "Come along now and I'll tuck you in."

Linda gave Drew a look that said she didn't think he should argue. Then crossing the room, she climbed into her bed.

The two boys said a quick good-night and crossed the hall to their room.

Amy was still crying quietly in Jed's arms when Thelma returned. "The least you could do is talk to Emily," the housekeeper said in lowered tones, standing near the rocking chair, looking down at the child with sympathetic concern. "She probably has a much better idea of what these kids are going through than any of us."

"Miss Mommy," Amy murmured between sobs.

"And, like I said before, they need someone to mother them, someone responsible and young enough to keep up with them," Thelma finished.

"I'll think about it," Jed conceded, hoping to stop Thelma's nagging.

"I want your word you'll do more than think about it," she insisted. "I want your word that you'll talk to her."

Jed was too tired to argue. "All right, all right!"

"Good!" Thelma smiled triumphantly. "Now, do you want me to rock Amy for a while?"

Amy's hands tightened around Jed's arm as if she was afraid he might give her up.

"No, I'll stay with her," he said gently.

Thelma nodded and quietly left the room.

"Who's Emily?" a small voice questioned from the other side of the room. "Is she going to come look after us like Nora?"

Jed turned to where Linda lay in her bed. The word "no" formed on his tongue but instead he heard himself say, "I don't know. We'll have to wait and see."

"I hope she's nice like Nora," Linda said hopefully.

"She's not exactly like Nora. But don't worry. We'll find someone you all will like." He didn't see how Emily could possibly work out and he was angry with himself for agreeing to talk to her. But right now he had Amy to worry about. Tomorrow he would worry about keeping his promise to Thelma.

* * *

Emily Hartley sat in the comfortable old wooden rocking chair on her front porch. In her hands was a now cool cup of coffee. Her feet were propped up on the wooden railing that lined the porch as she watched the sun rising over the trees in the distance. Here in northern Missouri, a slight winter chill still lingered in the March air. But the morning promised to be clear, and beyond the chill was the sweet smell of spring. However, the beauty and peacefulness of her surroundings did nothing to erase the frown from her face.

"Twenty-seven," she informed Harrington, the old half collie, half German shepherd who lay nearby. "I'm twenty-seven. I've lived here in Randolph's Well all my life. *And*, as far as I can see, all I've got in my future if I stay here is this farm and a tractor I have to cajole into working."

Harrington continued to rest his head on his front paws and watch her with his large watery dark eyes.

"Maybe I should sell this place and move to the city. I could go to secretarial school. At least it would be a change."

Harrington's ears pricked up. Shifting his gaze from Emily, he lifted his head and peered toward the rail fence that lined the yard. A rabbit was near one of the posts.

"A great help you are," she chastised with a pout. "Here I'm trying to tell you about this life crisis I'm going through and you let some dumb animal you don't even know draw your attention away."

The rabbit hopped off. Harrington laid his head back down on his paws and looked at her once again with a sorrowful expression.

Emily stared at the horizon. "Maybe the real problem is that the only living thing I've got to talk to is an old dog who doesn't even know what I'm talking about." She glanced at Harrington. "No offense meant."

He issued a gentle sound from deep down in his throat as if to say that no offense was taken.

Drawing a tired sigh, Emily lifted her feet off the porch rail. "But until I decide what to do with the rest of my life, guess I'd better get busy running this farm."

She was on her feet when the sound of a vehicle caught her attention. She looked down the gravel drive that led from the main road to the house and saw a red pickup coming toward her. It was one with an elongated cab. Jed Sawyer, she mused. He'd bought the new truck to accommodate his newly acquired family. Watching him park in the circular drive in front of the house, she wondered what he could possibly want from her.

Unexpectedly, she found herself admitting that he wasn't bad looking in a rugged sort of way. In fact, he had the kind of looks that appealed to a great many women. But he'd never appealed to her. She'd been looking for a man who was interested in settling down and Jed had never shown any inclination in that direction. Now he had four kids to raise. Must be quite a shock to him, she decided, noting the tired circles under his eyes. They were green eyes, the color of emeralds. A small shiver ran along her spine. It wasn't an unpleasant shiver—just a bit disconcerting. But then she'd always found Jed Sawyer a bit disconcerting.

"Morning," he said, coming around the truck toward her.

"Morning," she replied in a noncommittal tone, neither friendly nor hostile, but guarded, as she'd learned to be since the accident.

She felt him watching her as she descended the porch steps. The accident had left her with a limp. She'd worked hard to teach herself to ignore the reaction of others to it, but under his gaze she suddenly felt awkward. Her eyes traveled downward over her bulky plaid flannel shirt to her worn jeans and dusty Western-cut boots. Her long brown hair was pulled starkly back from her face and braided into a single pigtail that hung down her back. It was a plain simple style, practical for working the farm. Unexpectedly she found herself thinking that there was very little that was feminine about her appearance. Not that she didn't have the right curves in the right places. They just weren't easily discernible in her present attire and there was no sexy swing to her walk. Shocked to discover herself considering her lack of feminine appeal, she scowled. What Jed Sawyer thought of her as a woman was unimportant. "Sorry about your brother and his wife," she said.

He had stopped when he was about four feet from her, and now they stood facing one another. "Thanks."

Emily studied him. He was not an easy man to read. But although his manner was polite, she had the distinct impression that he was uncomfortable about being there. If her mother had been alive, by now she'd have invited him inside for a cup of coffee. But her mother wasn't alive and Emily had learned it wasn't smart for a woman alone to invite a man inside before knowing his full intentions. "To what do I owe this visit?" she asked when the pause in their conversation suddenly threatened to lengthen into a silence.

Jed's manner took on a grim edge. "Guess you've heard that I've got my brother's children."

Emily nodded. Jed's parents were dead and the other set of grandparents had disowned their daughter when she'd married Jed's brother. Jed was the only real family the children had. He'd been named guardian in his brother's will and had taken the children into his home. Again she found herself having difficulty picturing him in the role of father. "Guess they're a handful, especially for a bachelor."

"Yeah," he admitted. "And Thelma's getting a little too old to keep up with four youngsters."

Emily's brow wrinkled in confusion. "I heard you had Nora Randel looking after them."

Jed shrugged. "She quit yesterday." His jaw tensed. "It wasn't the kids. Her boyfriend didn't like her living out at my place and she hadn't expected to have to work so hard. Four kids take a lot of looking after. The job also required helping Thelma with the added wash and housecleaning, too."

Emily noticed him shift uneasily. It was obvious this small talk was getting on his nerves. It was even more obvious he would have preferred to be anywhere else but there with her. Her back muscles tightened defensively. "This might be easier on both of us if you'd just tell me why you're here so we can both get back to taking care of our own business."

"Truth is, the kids need someone who'd be stable, someone who doesn't mind hard work and who wouldn't leave on a whim or a moment's notice." Jed scowled introspectively. "I'd plan to lead into this more diplomatically but I'm not good with words. I'm here because Thelma suggested you might consider taking the job. She says you're real good with kids.''

Emily watched as his hand went up and rubbed the back of his neck as if just getting the words out had caused it to stiffen painfully.

"You must be desperate to have come here," she observed sarcastically. "It's obvious you don't agree with Thelma's assessment."

Jed hooked his thumbs through the loops on his jeans and frowned at her. "I just figured you wouldn't want to do it, but I gave Thelma my word I'd speak to you."

The barrier Emily had built around herself since the accident grew even more impenetrable. "Do you think that just because I can't have kids of my own, I don't like them?"

Jed continued to regard her coolly. "I don't know," he replied honestly. "You've never been an easy woman for me to read. But since the accident you seem to have become cold and withdrawn. The children need someone with a warm gentle touch. Thelma seems to think you still have that, but I'm not so sure."

The picture he painted of her hurt, but Emily refused to allow him to see that. "And so you just came over here to toss around a few insults to start my day off right?" she asked dryly.

Again he rubbed his neck. "This was a mistake," he said with gruff apology. "I didn't mean to come here and say anything that would upset you. It's just that you have a way of making a man nervous staring at him the way you do, as if you expect him to turn into a snake at any moment." The scowl on his face deepened. "I know life has dealt you a few hard blows, but it ain't healthy to go through it hating half the population.''

"I don't hate half the population," she snapped. "I just don't trust them." Her stomach knotted. She hadn't talked to anyone about her feelings since the accident and here she was shouting them at Jed Sawyer. "Look, I've got a farm to run. I'm sure you can find someone else who'll suit you a whole lot better than me to play nursemaid to your kids." Abruptly she turned and moved toward the house.

Behind her, she heard him utter a curse under his breath, and as she entered the house, she heard the door of his truck slam shut.

She moved over to the window. Hidden by the curtain, Emily watched him drive away. The muscles in her face hurt as she fought to keep her mask of indifference in place. Good riddance, she told herself, but down deep inside there was no feeling of relief. The truth was that she knew that, behind his rough exterior, Jed Sawyer had a decent heart. When she'd been laid up in the hospital all those weeks, he'd been among the group of farmers who had voluntarily harvested her crops and seen that her livestock was taken care of.

Walking into the hall, she glanced at herself in the mirror and suddenly froze. The face that stared back at her was rigid and cold. She couldn't blame him for thinking she was bitter. Her expression was that of the stereotypical prune-faced spinster from an old movie. Was this what the wall she had built around herself had done to her? If so, she didn't like it.

Suddenly the images of Jed's nieces and nephews filled her mind. She'd seen them in church with him. And she'd seen the frightened, sort of haunted look that came into their eyes every once in a while. She remembered that feeling well. "Wasn't I just saying I needed a change in my life?" she asked Harrington.

He let out a low howl as if in confirmation.

Chapter Two

Thelma wasn't able to hide her surprise when she answered the door. "Jed said you wouldn't be coming," she said as she stepped aside to allow Emily to enter. Her boss's angry expression was still vivid in the housekeeper's mind. He'd come back an hour ago, told her what had happened, then gone off to finish his plowing. Since then she'd been busy baking his favorite dessert and planning his favorite dinner in the hope of making up for the uncomfortable situation she'd put him in that morning.

"I didn't see any harm in coming over and meeting the children," Emily replied. "Thought if we got along I might take the job." She nodded toward the screen door. Harrington had already found himself a comfortable spot on the porch and was lying down, lazily taking in the scenery. Emily smiled sheepishly. "I have to admit, I'm getting tired of one-sided conversations with Harrington."

Thelma smiled. "It's about time you realized that." Taking Emily's hand, she started leading her through the house. "Come along. The children are in the den."

Emily suddenly had butterflies fluttering frantically around in her stomach. On the way over here she'd told herself that if the children didn't like her it wouldn't matter. At least she would have given the situation a chance. But now she was forced to admit that she wanted them to like her.

As she and Thelma entered the den, the children immediately forgot their television show and studied her with interest. But when Thelma introduced her their expressions became anxious, and they stared at her as if she had a third eye in the middle of her forehead.

"That's no way to greet a guest," Thelma admonished.

Linda scooted off the couch and stood regarding Emily with a frown. "She's the one Uncle Jed called the Ice Queen, isn't she?"

Thelma turned toward Emily apologetically. "Jed was a little hot under the collar when he got back."

"I don't blame him," Emily said, then added self-consciously, "I wasn't exactly at my most polite." Turning back toward the child, she said encouragingly, "It warmed up outside and I sort of melted."

Watching the four serious faces continuing to regard her dubiously, Emily was about to decide she had made a big mistake coming here. Then Drew rose and came to stand beside his sister.

"You here to take the job of taking care of us?" he asked.

Watching him, it occurred to Emily that he seemed much too serious for a child of nine. But then he'd been through a lot. "I thought we should see how we get along first," she replied.

"We're very easy to take care of," Linda assured her anxiously. "We won't be a bother. We promise."

The other three children all nodded in agreement.

"Be good," Amy promised, looking pleadingly up at Emily.

The children appeared to be a great deal more willing to have her take the job than their uncle had been, Emily mused.

"What the devil!" Jed muttered as he rounded the side of the house. Emily Hartley was playing catch with his nephews while his nieces were sitting on the porch with Harrington, petting the old dog and talking to him as if he were a long-lost friend.

"Uncle Jed!" Drew yelled out happily, losing interest in the game and running toward his uncle.

Emily's muscles stiffened as she turned to face the farmer. His grim expression told her he wasn't exactly delighted to find her there.

"Emily's not nearly as bad as you think," Drew announced as he reached the man.

"Yeah, she melted," Dennis informed him.

Jed smiled down at the boys, but Emily noticed that the smile didn't reach his eyes. "Why don't you children go inside and tell Thelma that your uncle is home for lunch," she suggested in a voice that was more of a command than a request.

"Linda and Amy can," Drew replied, obviously not wanting to miss what was said between his uncle and the Ice Queen.

"All of you," Jed ordered sternly.

Drew glanced anxiously from one adult to the other, but obeyed.

"You want to tell me why you're here?" Jed asked as soon as he and Emily were alone.

"I thought I should apologize for my behavior this morning," she replied self-consciously. "Guess I'm a bit defensive."

"A bit," he conceded, continuing to study her narrowly. "Is that all you came about?"

Emily's throat tightened. Obviously this had been a mistake. He'd changed his mind about considering her for the job. Pride came to her rescue and her shoulders straightened. "You could be a bit more forgiving. I did apologize."

Taking off his Stetson, Jed wiped the sweat from his forehead on the sleeve of his shirt. "Sorry," he said, but the word lacked remorse. Tersely he added, "I'm tired and that's making me cranky."

He smelled of sweat and freshly turned earth and she saw the exhaustion etched into his face. Under the circumstances it was understandable that he should be short-tempered. A sudden shock swept through her. She was actually making an excuse for a man's behavior! The urge to leave was strong, but glancing toward the house, she saw the children bunched together at the screen door watching. They needed someone to take care of them and she needed someone to care about before she dried up inside. Her gaze returned to Jed. "The children and I seem able to get along just fine. I was wondering if the job offer was still open."

For a moment he regarded her in a stony silence. Then he said honestly, "I'm not sure this will work out. But I'm desperate." His gaze narrowed challengingly. "However, I don't want someone who's going to leave the moment the going gets tough."

"I don't desert my commitments just because of a little stormy weather," she replied. His gaze narrowed further and she mentally kicked herself. She knew he was recalling what Howard Parker had done to her and that made what she'd just said sound like sour grapes. The truth was that she was glad she had discovered Howard's true nature before she'd married him.

For a moment longer Jed continued to hesitate, then said with a dubious scowl, "I guess you're hired."

Her pride almost caused Emily to tell him she'd changed her mind. It was obvious he didn't really want her here. But playing with the children had given her a feeling of warmth she hadn't experienced in too long a time. In a businesslike tone she said, "I'll need to find someone to oversee my farm. I've already plowed and fertilized half of it. I wouldn't want to see the work or money wasted, and there's a bit of livestock that will need tending."

Jed glanced toward the door where the children remained clustered as if he needed some reassurance he was doing the right thing. Returning his attention to Emily, his jaw set itself into a firm line. "I can see that your place is taken care of. When do you want to start?"

In spite of Jed's openly spoken reservations, Emily felt a surge of joy. But, for the past four years, she'd spent a great deal of energy keeping her feelings to herself and so outwardly she remained cool. "I guess today's as good a time as any."

Again Jed frowned as if he was certain he'd made a mistake, then said, "Today's fine. I'll have Thelma show you to your room." As he started toward the house, Emily caught up with him.

Stopping him with a hand on his arm, she stared up at him. "My room?"

He frowned impatiently. "It's a live-in job. You know that."

"I knew that Nora lived here," she replied, realizing she hadn't thought this whole thing through thoroughly. A heat beneath her hand caused her to realize she was still touching him. Shocked by how aware she was of the contact, she released him abruptly. "But I figured I could come in early and leave late. I'm not that far away."

"Amy, especially, needs twenty-four-hour care. At one time or another they've all had nightmares. I'm hiring you for a full-time job and that means being available twenty-four hours a day." Challenge again flickered in the green depths of his eyes. "You don't have to worry about me," he assured her dryly. "I'm not going to bother you."

His assurance should have eased her mind, but instead it had the sting of an insult. *I'm just nervous*, she told herself. Harrington had risen and wandered down the porch steps to join them. A sudden rush of concern swept over her. "Harrington will have to stay, too," she stipulated.

Reaching down, Jed petted the dog's head. "Ain't never minded Harrington. He'll fit in just fine."

The dog's going to fit in just fine, but he's not sure I will, Emily thought as she followed him into the house. Well, she'd show him!

"Are you going to let her stay?" Drew asked as the children stepped back to allow Jed and Emily to enter the house.

"Yes," he replied.

Emily had expected the children to accept her without protest since they had gotten along so well during the morning. What she hadn't expected to see were the glances of relief that passed among them.

Thelma gave Jed a triumphant grin, then turned her attention to Emily. "I set you a place at the table."

Emily hesitated. "If I'm going to start today, maybe I should go home and pack."

"Linda and I can come and help," Drew said with an authority that reminded Emily of his uncle.

"Me, too," Dennis piped up.

"Me, too," Amy mimicked.

They all looked so eager, Emily couldn't keep from smiling. "In that case we should all eat a hearty lunch."

The children nodded, their expressions serious and headed toward the dining room.

"You'll have to take my truck," Jed said, tossing her the keys. "There's a car seat for Amy in it and seat belts for the rest of the kids."

Emily stood looking at the keys dangling in her hand. This morning she had only herself to think about; this afternoon she had four children. *I just hope I haven't bitten off more than I can chew,* she prayed. Glancing up, she was met by a pair of shuttered green eyes. *He thinks I have. Well, he's wrong!* She forced a confident smile. "Thanks," she said, tossing the keys into the air and catching them in a nonchalant manner as she preceded him into the dining room.

Several times during the meal, she felt a prickling on her neck and glanced toward Jed to find him watching her. The uncertainty was still in his eyes.

As they all left the house following the meal, he glanced toward the truck then toward the sky. "I'd go with you but I've still got a few acres left to plow," he muttered. "And it looks like rain."

Emily couldn't believe her ears. He had actually been considering accompanying them. He sounded and acted like a mother hen. She was tempted to assure him that she was perfectly capable of taking care of the children and to point out that he had hired her for that purpose. But instead she said simply, "I'm sure we can handle this on our own." She couldn't fault his protective attitude toward the children. It was clear he honestly cared about them. A lot of men in his position would have resented having four children thrust on them.

"I'd better show you how to use Amy's car seat," he said, continuing to hesitate.

Emily watched him lifting the children into the cab and making certain each was properly secured. Then she stood silently while he demonstrated how to fasten Amy in properly. "I'm sure I can handle it," she said, as he continued to linger beside the cab.

He didn't look convinced, but he nodded and headed toward the barn.

She expected a lot of squirming or at least some giggling and talking as she drove, but the children sat quietly. Like little adults, she thought, then corrected herself—more like mannequins.

At the house, they all filed in after her. Picking up Amy, she carried her up the stairs while the others followed. But as she found her suitcase and began loading in her clothes, she discovered that having four pairs of eyes watching her every move was disconcerting. "I've got some milk and cookies in the kitchen," she said. "You didn't have any desert at lunch. Want some?"

The three younger children glanced at Drew. His mouth formed a grim pout as if he was considering all the consequences, then he nodded. Immediately the other three turned to Emily and nodded, also.

Very quickly she had them all sitting at her table with milk and cookies. Satisfied they were safe, she went back upstairs to finish packing. She had snapped a second suitcase closed with the finality of one who felt she had packed enough when she heard an unhappy squeal from downstairs. Racing to the kitchen, she found Linda and Drew mopping up a spilt glass of milk while Amy and Dennis looked on in horror.

"It was an accident," Linda said quickly, her face paling as she looked up and saw Emily. "Amy saw Drew dunking his cookie..." She paused to toss her brother an impatient glance, then returned her attention to Emily and finished, "And she wanted to try it."

"A little spilt milk isn't a problem," Emily assured them, shocked by the anxiousness on their faces. She knew Thelma. The housekeeper had a heart of gold, especially where children were concerned. It didn't make any sense that these four should be so frightened of retribution for a simple accident.

"Then you won't quit?" Drew asked.

Tears had begun to well up in Amy's eyes and now small sobs were coming from her. Lifting the child into her arms, Emily gently stroked her cheek. "It's really all right. I'm not angry. It was just an accident."

"Amy, don't cry," Linda ordered in a worried voice. "Honestly, she doesn't cry much," she added to Emily. "We're really very easy to take care of."

"We want to stay together," Dennis suddenly announced.

"Of course you do," Emily replied, startled by this unexpected statement.

"If you don't stay we might get split—" Dennis continued grimly.

"Hush!" Drew ordered and Dennis shut up.

Emily's gaze traveled from face to face and she saw the fear in their eyes. "Why don't you tell me what this is all about?" she suggested, kneeling so that she was eye level with them.

Linda and Dennis again both turned to Drew for leadership. "Last night I heard Uncle Jed on the phone," he said. "I wasn't eavesdropping," he injected defensively. "I was just on the stairs when he answered it."

"I'm sure you weren't purposely eavesdropping," Emily assured him.

"Anyway, it was Grandma Cramer."

Emily had to admit she was surprised that Vivian Cramer had any contact with Jed. Vivian had been so set against her daughter's marriage to Jed's brother, she hadn't spoken to her daughter since the elopement. And according to everything Emily had heard, the woman had not even recognized the births of her grandchildren. "Go on," she encouraged when Drew's pause threatened to lengthen into a silence.

"She heard about Nora leaving," he continued grimly. "She volunteered to take Linda and Amy." He frowned self-consciously. "I don't think she likes Dennis and me."

Emily couldn't believe anyone would consider splitting up these children. It was so obvious that they depended on one another for support. "Surely your uncle didn't agree."

"He said he was going to keep trying to find someone to look after us," Drew conceded, then added worriedly, "But he didn't say he wouldn't give the girls to her if he couldn't find someone who would stay."

"We won't go!" Linda stated emphatically, reaching out and taking hold of Drew's hand.

In her mind's eye Emily recalled the caring concern on Jed's face when he was buckling up the children in the cab of the truck. It had seemed genuine. But it was hard to tell with men, she reminded herself. "Don't you worry," she soothed. "I plan to stay and take care of you."

The children calmed down, but during the rest of the day Emily noticed that they remained tense. A part of her was tempted to talk to Jed Sawyer. But a stronger part was afraid she might hear something she didn't want to hear. She really didn't know the man well enough to predict how he would react and she couldn't shake the feeling that maybe he was getting tired of being an instant father.

The rain started late in the afternoon. Jed hadn't returned, and Emily guessed he'd gotten caught in the middle of his plowing. When he came in about an hour later, she knew she'd been right. He was soaked to the skin, his jeans and shirt plastered to his body. A very masculine body, Emily thought watching him as he stood on the porch kicking off his muddy boots. She felt a stirring deep inside and, scowling at herself, she turned her attention back to the interior of the house. Now was not the time to suddenly discover that she could still be attracted to a man, and Jed Sawyer was most definitely not a man she wanted to be attracted to.

As Jed started toward the stairs, he suddenly let out a loud howl. Cursing gruffly under his breath, he leaned against the wall and rubbed the bottom of his foot. On the floor was a tiny truck. "Who the devil left this toy in the hall?" he demanded.

Drew immediately rushed out with Dennis close behind.

"I didn't mean to, Uncle Jed," Dennis apologized.

"I told you to be more careful with your toys," Drew admonished his brother, panic in his voice.

"I'm sorry." Tears were filling Dennis's eyes now.

"I'm sure your uncle understands," Emily said, coming to the children's rescue.

"Yeah, sure." Jed was watching Dennis in confusion as the child suddenly dissolved into tears. "It's no big deal," he assured the boy. "Beats the time I stepped on a rattler."

Dennis's tears slowed as he looked up at his uncle.

"Go on back and play," Jed directed. "I've got to get into dry clothes."

But as he started up the stairs, Emily watched the children. The anxious look in their eyes had grown.

"Let's get all the toys put away," Drew ordered, and immediately all four, even Amy, began to straighten up the den.

When Jed came back down, the room was neat and tidy and the children were seated quietly watching television. They all greeted him with cheerful polite faces, but their eyes were guarded. Linda quickly got up and brought him his newspaper.

Emily found it close to painful to watch the children trying so hard to behave like perfect little adults.

She saw Amy begin to scoot out of her chair and head toward Jed. Immediately Linda put a restraining hand on her sister's arm and shook her head. Worry showed in Amy's eyes and she snuggled into the corner of the overstuffed chair like a street urchin on a cold night.

Emily glanced toward Jed. He was watching the children with a look of puzzlement on his face.

"Dinner's served," Thelma announced.

Instead of making a dash for the table, the children quietly got up and walked sedately into the dining room.

Still looking confused, Jed scooped up Amy and carried her into the dining room. At the table, they all sat like frozen mannequins until Jed had said grace, then they carefully passed around the food.

"How was your afternoon?" Jed said, breaking the tense silence hovering over the table.

"It was fine," Drew replied for himself and the others.

"You're all especially quiet this evening," Thelma remarked as she brought out a platter of hot biscuits and set them on the table.

"I was sort of getting used to at least one squabble," Jed remarked.

"We haven't meant to be a problem to you," Drew replied with apology in his voice. "From now on we'll be good."

"You've been just fine so far," Jed assured him. "I never expected perfection."

But still the children maintained their very proper demeanor. Something had to be done before this went much further, Emily decided. Mentally she practiced ways of approaching Jed. Feeling a prickling on her neck, she glanced up and found him watching her.

There was anger in his eyes as if he blamed her for this change in his nieces and nephews, and her chin lifted defiantly. As she turned back to her food, she caught the sudden fear in Drew's eyes. He'd noticed the unspoken exchange.

"We're very fond of Emily," the boy said. "I'm certain she will take very good care of us."

Jed merely nodded and an even heavier silence fell over the table.

The children ate very little. When they refused pieces of Thelma's chocolate cake, the expression of impatience on Jed's face increased. "You all go into the den and watch television," he ordered them. Turning to Emily, he said, "I want to speak to you in my study."

She watched the children glancing nervously over their shoulders as she followed Jed from the dining room. Her heart went out to them.

At the study door, he paused to allow her to enter first. Following her in, he kicked the door shut with the heel of his boot and stood glaring at her. "I want to know what you've done to those kids!"

"I haven't done anything," she replied levelly.

"Well, I sure as blue blazes haven't," he growled. "And don't try to tell me that they're acting normal, because they aren't. They're all stiff and nervous."

Emily didn't think she'd ever seen a man so angry. Under other circumstances, she admitted, she might even have cowered under the intensity of his glare, but her concern for the children kept her from wavering. "They're trying to be perfect so you won't split them up."

Indignation mingled with his anger. "Split them up? Where in the world would they get that idea—" He stopped. "They overheard my conversation with Vivian last night," he muttered.

Now it was Emily's turn to show indignation. "I can't believe you would even consider splitting them up," she said curtly. "They depend on one another for support. They've lost their parents and now they are clinging together because they're afraid of losing one another."

He scowled at her. "Of course, I wouldn't consider splitting them up."

"Apparently you weren't that emphatic over the phone," she pointed out, recalling the fear in the children's eyes.

Jed raked a hand through his hair in an agitated fashion. "I was feeling desperate and Vivian was only suggesting that the girls come stay with her for a couple of weeks. I told her I'd have to think about it. Afterwards I realized I couldn't allow it. She never showed any interest in the children until her daughter was killed and now she only wants to recognize the existence of the girls. That's not healthy." The anger returned to his eyes and he again leveled his gaze upon Emily. "Why didn't you tell me this when I came in?"

"I didn't have a chance," she replied in her defense. "Besides, I didn't know if you were getting tired of having the children and looking for a way of getting rid of them."

His jaw tensed and a possessive protectiveness etched itself into his features. "Those children are my family. I would never consider getting rid of them."

Emily suddenly found herself wondering what it would feel like to have him feel that way about her. *Someone* to feel that way about her, she corrected.

"Maybe you should go and assure them that you have no intention of allowing them to be split up," she told him.

Jed nodded. But as he started out the door, he paused with his hand on the knob and turned back toward her. "From now on you will tell me immediately about anything that's bothering them," he ordered. Before she had a chance to reply he was gone.

Emily followed but waited in the hall outside the den until he had assured the children that they did not need to worry about being split up. When she entered the room, she found him on the couch with Amy and Dennis in his lap and Linda and Drew seated on either side of him. There was a tenderness in his eyes that shook her. She'd never pictured him as a family man. But there he was looking like the perfect father with a bevy of children he adored.

The urge to be a part of that quintet on the couch filled her. *You're the hired help,* she reminded herself. *And you'd better keep that in mind.* "I think I'll go up and unpack," she said, easing herself back out the door.

They barely noticed her exit as Jed began to tickle Drew, and suddenly there was a free-for-all on the couch.

"Nice little ready-made family Jed's got there."

Emily jerked around to find Thelma behind her. "Yes," she agreed.

Thelma peeked around her into the den. "All they need now is a mother."

"Guess they'll just have to settle for me for the moment," Emily replied absently, as she listened to the laughter from the den and wished she could have stayed and been a part of it. But she would have felt like an interloper.

"You'll do just fine," Thelma said with a bright smile. "Think I'll go in and see if they want that cake now."

A few minutes later as she unpacked in the privacy of her room, it suddenly dawned on Emily that if and when Jed did marry, she would be out of a job. *Don't get too close,* she warned herself. *You're only temporary.*

Chapter Three

It was not going to be an easy promise to keep, she admitted later that evening as she finished giving Amy her bath and dressed the child for bed. Linda had hovered in the shadows the entire time. Both girls seemed so vulnerable that Emily had to fight not to put her arms around them and hug them protectively.

But it was Dennis who provided her with her first real challenge of the day. When she went to collect him for his bath, he shied away.

Drew spoke up quickly in his brother's defense. "I can help him with his bath—he's just a little shy."

Jed had fallen asleep in a chair and they were all speaking in lowered voices so as not to disturb him. Emily was trying to decide on the best way to handle this problem when a groggy male voice said, "I'll oversee these two hooligans. We men have to stick together."

Glancing over her shoulder, Emily saw Jed levering himself out of the chair. He looked exhausted, but there was a gentleness in his eyes that told her he didn't mind taking care of the boys.

Going back upstairs, she read the girls a couple of stories and was tucking them into bed when Jed came in to say goodnight.

"Dennis is in bed," he informed her as they left the girls' room, "but I let Drew stay up a little longer."

Emily nodded. She didn't like admitting that any man could cause her to feel uneasy, but standing there in the hall with Jed Sawyer did. She was just tired, she told herself. Still, the urge to escape was too strong to resist. "I'll go in and say good night to Dennis and then go down and see if I can give Thelma a hand," she said, turning and heading toward the boys' room. For the first few steps she felt his eyes on her, then she heard him turn and walk toward the stairs.

Jed was in his study when she went back downstairs. Where he was shouldn't matter, she told herself. But she was glad she wouldn't be running into him. *You're being childish,* she chided herself. *He's merely a man.*

In the kitchen she found Thelma sitting at the table working the crossword puzzle from the evening paper. "They're good children, don't you think?" Thelma said as Emily poured herself a cup of coffee and joined the housekeeper.

"Very good," Emily agreed.

Thelma frowned and studied her closely. "I thought I heard a note of hesitation." She smiled encouragingly. "I know it's a lot of work to look after them. But you'll get used to it."

"It's not the children," Emily said, then flushed when Thelma regarded her even more closely. Shrugging as if to say she hadn't meant anything important, she finished levelly, "It's just that Jed's been a real surprise. I never pictured him as a family man."

Thelma's smile returned. "I always knew he had it in him. All he needed was the right incentive to bring it out."

"I suppose," Emily conceded, her gaze traveling around the homey kitchen. She'd expected to feel somewhat uncomfortable, at least for a little while, living in a house with other people again. She'd grown used to her solitude. But she didn't feel uncomfortable, and she was forced to admit that she'd missed this kind of friendly family atmosphere. She'd just never expected to find it in Jed Sawyer's house.

She helped Thelma with the crossword puzzle for a few minutes, then the exhaustion of the day caught up with her and she excused herself to go to bed. But before going upstairs, she went out onto the front porch to check on Harrington. Like her own front porch, this one ran the full length of the front of the two-story frame farmhouse. It had four steps leading up to it and a wooden railing along the edge. Harrington had found a comfortable niche in a corner. Jed had offered the old dog the comfort of the screened-in porch at the back of the house, but when the weather was good, Harrington preferred the open air. Squatting, Emily ran her hand along his neck and ruffled the fur on his head. "Quite a change, huh boy?"

Harrington simply shifted his head into a more comfortable position.

"You never were much of a conversationalist," she chided gently, ruffling his fur again. "Just don't get too comfortable," she advised, talking more to herself than to Harrington. "Our boss isn't so certain we're right for this job and I have a feeling that should he find any other option we're going to be out of here on our proverbial ear."

"You seem to be working out better than I thought you would."

Startled, Emily glanced up to see Jed through the porch railing. "It's not nice to sneak up on people like that," she admonished as he strode around the porch and mounted the steps.

"Sorry," he apologized without any real remorse. "Had to go check on a few things down by the barn. I didn't mean to scare you."

He made her sound like a skittish child. "You didn't *scare* me," she corrected. "You *startled* me."

"I didn't mean to *startle* you then," he conceded with a note of amusement.

The hairs on the back of her neck bristled. He was making fun of her. *He's only teasing you a little,* her more rational side pointed out. *Don't overreact.* The wall of reserve she had built around her emotions came firmly into place. "Guess I'll be getting inside," she said, beginning to rise. Suddenly a sharp pain shot down her leg. She gasped and her jaw tensed as she held back a cry.

Unexpectedly two strong hands closed around her waist and she felt herself being lifted to her feet. "You all right?" Jed asked with concern.

Emily flushed with embarrassment. "Every once in a while my hip decides to give me trouble," she muttered. But it wasn't her hip that was occupying her mind at the moment. Jed was holding her from behind and his breath was stirring the hairs on the back of her neck, causing a curious tingling sensation to spread over her shoulders. But it was the two large callused hands surrounding her waist that were the most disconcerting. Their touch was warm and the heat of the contact was spreading rapidly through her. "I'm really all right now," she assured him. "You can let go."

He regarded her dubiously. "You sure?"

Emily's jaw tensed. The last thing she wanted from him or anyone was pity. "I'm not an invalid," she replied curtly. "I just moved wrong."

Immediately he released her as if he'd suddenly found himself holding a live rattler. "I was only trying to be helpful," he growled.

Emily drew a deep breath and turned to face him. "Sorry," she apologized self-consciously. The glances of pity she had grown so used to filled her mind. "I guess I'm getting sick and tired of the way people treat me—as if having a limp makes me less than capable." Realizing she'd spoken aloud, she flushed again. That was the second time today she'd let thoughts she'd kept only to herself come out. *Maybe I've been keeping them in too long,* she mused. But Jed Sawyer was not the person she would have chosen to voice them to.

"I can understand that," he was saying.

Suddenly afraid that he might start thinking she couldn't physically handle the job of caring for his nieces and nephews, she added, "I can move as well as most people, just a bit more awkwardly."

"I never thought you couldn't," he replied. He shifted uneasily, then hooked his thumbs in the pockets of his jeans. "I wanted to apologize for losing my temper with you earlier."

She hadn't expected him to apologize. But as she'd told Thelma, he'd been surprising her quite a bit today. "I should have tried to speak to you sooner," she admitted.

"I know I haven't been very encouraging, but I do hope this works out," he continued, now in businesslike tones.

Night had fallen fully and only the moon and stars gave any light. Standing on the porch with his hat on, Jed's face was in shadow and she couldn't see his features. Still, she was acutely aware of his gaze upon her and a nervousness spread through her. *You've kept to yourself too long,* she chided mentally. *You can't even stand on a porch in the dark talking to a man without getting tense.* She ordered herself to relax but it didn't work. "It's been a long day," she said, giving in to the desire to escape. "Guess I'll be saying good night."

"Night," he replied, moving toward the door and holding it open for her.

She brushed against his arm as she passed him. It was hard as granite, but it was the heat that again trailed through her that set her nerves on edge.

But as she started up the stairs and heard him coming behind her, she had to fight to keep from jogging to her room. When she reached the landing, and headed down the hall she heard him open a door. Glancing covertly over her shoulder, she saw him entering the first room on the other side of the stairs, and for the first time, she realized how close they all were up here. *You could be a million miles away for all the interest he has in you,* she reminded herself. *It doesn't matter where he sleeps.*

But later that night, she wasn't so certain. She awoke around two to the sound of someone moving around in the girls' room. Going in to investigate, she found Linda sitting in the rocking chair, holding her doll and looking lost and frightened. "Is something wrong?" Emily asked, approaching the girl and gently combing a wayward strand of hair from the child's face with the tips of her fingers.

"I couldn't sleep," Linda replied, adding apologetically, "I'm sorry if I woke you."

"I was having a little trouble sleeping myself," Emily lied. "How about some milk and cookies? I'm sure Thelma won't mind if we raid her kitchen."

A small relieved smile played at the corners of the young girl's mouth. Nodding, she slid out of the chair and tiptoed to the door.

Down in the kitchen, Emily found some cookies and poured them each a glass of milk. "Does your doll have a name?" she asked, breaking the uncomfortable silence that threatened to settle between them.

"Belinda," Linda replied. A worried frown wrinkled the child's brow as she looked down at the doll in her arms. "She gets frightened sometimes and can't sleep."

The little blond-haired child looked so fragile. Emily sat down beside her and touched Linda's cheek lightly. "Everyone gets frightened at one time or another. But she's perfectly safe here."

"Yeah, I told her that," Linda replied. But she didn't look totally convinced. She picked up a cookie, then put it back uneaten on the plate and turned toward Emily. "Have you ever been afraid?"

Emily found herself recalling the day she had left the hospital and gone back to that empty farmhouse. The place had seemed so hollow and she'd felt terribly alone. She'd been afraid then. And there was the time Duncan Marlow had paid her a call. He was a couple of years older than her and divorced. She'd invited him in for coffee. That was when she'd learned it wasn't safe to invite a man in unless she knew his full intentions. He'd started making a strong advance toward her and she ended up threatening him with a fireplace poker. "Yes, there have been a few times," she admitted. Her jaw tensed. "But you can't let fear rule your life."

"Neither one of you has anything to be afraid of here." Jed's gruff tones suddenly sounded from behind them.

Startled, Emily swung around to find him standing at the kitchen door. He was dressed only in a pair of hastily pulled-on jeans. She'd seen men without their shirts on before, but the sight of his broad muscular chest with it's V of dark curly hair caused a very feminine, very unexpected rush of excitement to spread through her. *It's only because I'm in his kitchen in the middle of the night in my nightgown and robe,* she reasoned. *It's not natural for me to be in a strange man's house in the middle of the night. Any male would have affected me the same way.* "We didn't mean to wake you," she managed, and marveled at how calm she sounded.

"Two in the morning is always the best time for milk and cookies," he replied in an easy drawl. Glancing at a door on the far side of the room, he added, "But why don't we take them into the den so we don't wake up Thelma?"

Emily flushed. She'd forgotten the housekeeper had a suite of rooms off the kitchen. "I didn't think about that," she said, quickly rising and picking up the two glasses of milk. "I hope we didn't disturb her."

"She's slept through a lot more commotion than this," Jed assured her, picking up the plate of cookies.

Linda yawned. "I think Belinda's ready to go back to bed," she announced.

"Then why don't I escort you and Belinda back upstairs?" Jed suggested with a grin. Setting the cookie plate back on the table, he lifted the little girl into his arms and strode toward the door.

A moment later, Emily found herself alone in the kitchen still holding the two glasses of milk. To her chagrin she was feeling shaky, and the image of Jed's muscular form continued to linger in her mind. "I'm just not myself," she muttered. "Who would be at two in the morning?"

Being careful not to make any more noise than was necessary, she straightened up the kitchen and started back to her room. But as she reached the landing, Jed came out of the girls' room.

"Is she all tucked in for the night?" Emily asked, feeling a nervous need to say something.

"She's fine," he replied, studying her grimly. "Guess it's just going to take a little time for her insecurities to fade and for her to realize she'll always have a permanent home here."

Emily nodded. Again she found herself recalling her own fear and emptiness. "It's a shock to suddenly find yourself alone." His gaze narrowed and she realized that again she had revealed more of herself than she wanted to. Embarrassed, she added quickly, "Of course Linda isn't really alone. She has you and her brothers and sister. I'm sure her fears will fade eventually."

His scrutiny became more intense until she was afraid he could see right into her soul. She had to escape. Her back rigid, she turned away from him and started for her room. Suddenly his hand closed around her arm with a grip of iron and he brought her to an abrupt halt.

"There was no reason for you to face your loss alone, either," he said grimly. "It was your choice to shut yourself away from everyone else."

Emily drew a shaky breath and her back stiffened even more. "When I left the hospital my pride was all I had left. I'd lost my parents, I'd been disfigured and my fiancé had deserted me. When people looked at me they didn't know whether to be embarrassed for me or to pity me. Usually they settled for a combination of the two and I wasn't in the mood for either." Hot tears suddenly burned at the back of her eyes. Jerking free, she strode to her room. She could feel his eyes on her all the way. Even when she had entered and closed the door between them she could feel his presence.

Leaning against the wooden structure as if she felt the need to add her own strength to the barrier between them, she heard nothing for a long moment. Then the sound of his bare feet padding down the hall was followed by the sound of the door of his room closing.

The tears burned hotter. She had cried for her parents, but she hadn't cried over anything else that had happened to her since. She wasn't going to start now. Closing her eyes, she very carefully rebuilt the wall of reserve she'd worked so hard to keep in place around her emotions.

The next morning she awoke confident that she had herself and her emotions under tight control. It was five-thirty and dawn was breaking over the horizon. The children were still asleep.

She dressed quietly so as not to disturb them, then went downstairs in search of a cup of coffee. But as she entered the kitchen, she found Jed sitting at the kitchen table eating his breakfast. *Indifference is all you should feel,* she ordered herself. "Morning," she said politely.

"Morning," he replied. "Hope you got enough sleep."

His expression was unreadable but those green eyes of his unnerved her as he watched her walking across the room. "Yes, I got plenty," she assured him. *Indifference!* her inner voice screamed at her. *He's merely a man. A very masculine man,* she amended, her mind going back to the vision of him the night before without his shirt. *Stop it!* she ordered herself.

"Morning," Thelma greeted her, entering the kitchen.

Emily drew a breath of relief, then scowled at herself for feeling the need of a third party. "Morning," she returned, adding, "I hope we didn't disturb you last night."

"More like this morning," Thelma corrected, then grinned. "I heard you, but I figured you could handle it on your own, so I just rolled over and went back to sleep." Her smile broadened. "What can I fix you for breakfast?"

Emily recalled her mother asking that question in the same friendly mothering tone, and a lump formed in her throat. So much for having her emotions under control, she mused. Aloud she said, "I think I'll just have a cup of coffee now and eat with the children when they get up.''

Thelma nodded and poured her a mug.

As Emily added milk, Thelma asked Jed what his schedule for the day was so she could plan the meals. As they talked, the lump in Emily's throat grew. It was the same sort of discussion she and her mother and father used to have each morning. ''Think I'll go check on Harrington,'' she muttered and made a quick escape. Doubting that either of them had even noticed her retreat, she took her coffee with her when she went out onto the front porch.

The old dog was lying comfortably where she'd left him the night before. ''Morning, boy,'' she greeted him gently, the persistent lump still in her throat.

Lifting his head, he looked at her for a moment, then lazily lowered his head back onto his paws in a contented fashion.

''Guess I'm not used to human company so early in the morning,'' she said, squatting to pet him.

The sound of boots coming her way caused her to stiffen. She'd expected Jed to leave by the back door. As he came out onto the porch, she got up. ''You all right?'' he asked. ''Thelma said you looked a little pale when you left the kitchen.''

He was studying her with an intensity that caused the hairs on the back of her neck to prickle. ''For a minute Thelma reminded me of my mom.'' Damn! she couldn't believe she'd admitted that aloud. She forced a nonchalant shrug. ''Guess I'm not used to being around other people this early in the morning,'' she added, using the excuse she'd given Harrington.

He frowned. ''Shutting yourself away from others like you did wasn't healthy.''

A part of her wanted to tell him that she wasn't interested in his advice or opinions on her behavior. But instead she heard herself saying grudgingly, "I suppose you're right." The stunned expression on his face stopped her embarrassment at having again been more open than she'd ever intended.

But as the silence that had fallen between them continued, her uneasiness grew again. That she kept making these admissions to him unnerved her. The desire to put distance between herself and Jed was too strong to ignore. "I've been thinking about my position here," she said, forcing a businesslike quality into her voice. "Yesterday, I had my meals with you and the children. But I'm actually the hired help and I don't want to impose. It's occurred to me that I should be having my meals with Thelma in the kitchen."

For another long moment, he regarded her in silence, then he said firmly, "You'll eat with the children and me." Before she could protest, he left the porch and headed for the barn.

It doesn't matter where I eat or whom I eat with, she told herself as she watched his departing back. And she would stop making these embarrassing confessions.

The sound of young voices pushed Jed Sawyer to the back of her mind. Going inside she discovered all four of her charges on their way down the stairs.

As she sat eating breakfast with them, it suddenly dawned on her that she would be spending today and every day with them...but doing what? "How do you usually spend your days?" she asked, addressing her question to all of them.

Drew shrugged. "We watch television and play some."

"What about chores?" she asked, not wanting to plan anything that would interfere with their assigned duties.

Linda looked up at her with a puzzled expression. "We don't have any."

Behind the children Thelma frowned impatiently. "Jed wants them to relax and enjoy themselves." Still frowning, she added pointedly, "I'll go make up their beds while they finish breakfast."

"I can do that later," Emily said quickly as the housekeeper started toward the door. "The children are my responsibility."

With a shrug Thelma returned to the sink. But when the children left the kitchen a little later to go watch television and Emily went upstairs to make their beds, she discovered Thelma had followed her. Standing in the doorway of the girls' room watching Emily make Amy's bed, Thelma said, "I don't mind making beds, but it bothers me that these children aren't learning to be responsible for themselves."

Before Emily could respond, the housekeeper was on her way back downstairs.

Straightening, Emily stood looking at Linda's bed. Thelma was right. She went back downstairs to where the children were watching cartoons.

"It's time the three of you older children learned to make your own beds," she announced.

Four sets of eyes looked at her dubiously.

"My mother used to say if you sleep in it, you make it," Emily added.

Drew nodded. "Linda and I always made our beds at home," he admitted.

"This is your home now," Emily pointed out gently. "So how about making those beds?"

That haunted look passed through his eyes, then he nodded again, and waving to the others to follow him, he led the way up the stairs.

Emily helped Dennis while Amy watched.

Thelma entered the room as they completed their bed making. "Right nice job you kids did."

Linda smiled proudly, Drew looked as if it was what she should have expected, and Dennis frowned grudgingly as if he didn't like this new change in the rules.

"I always have a little garden near the house with tomatoes, peppers and a few other vegetables," Thelma said shifting her attention to Emily. "But the truth is my arthritis is bothering me a bit. I was wondering if you and the children could give me a hand."

Emily saw through the older woman's ploy, but she couldn't fault her. Emily herself was too farm bred to find it easy to watch the children lying around all day in front of the television. "We could do the job for you," she replied, adding encouragingly to the children, "can't we?"

"Sure," Drew replied enthusiastically while Amy and Linda nodded and Dennis looked skeptical.

By the time Jed came back to the house for lunch they had most of the earth turned. Emily had done the major portion of the heavy work. But she had found jobs for all the children. Linda had been assigned to watch Amy while Drew and Dennis had broken up large clumps of dirt with the hoe.

"We're going to work in the fertilizer this afternoon," Drew informed his uncle as they all sat at the table and began eating hungrily.

"Amy likes the earthworms," Linda interjected, screwing her face into a look of disgust.

"Earthworms," Amy echoed, smiling brightly.

"We made our beds, too," Dennis announced proudly.

"Sounds like you all had a busy morning," Jed replied with a smile, but when he turned toward Emily she could see that the smile didn't reach his eyes.

As they finished the meal and began to leave the table, he rose and faced her. "I want to speak to you in my study."

His expression was shuttered, but instinct told her she was in trouble. She sent the children into the den to watch television, then followed him down the hall.

Holding the door open for her, he waited until she had entered, then followed her and closed the door. But as he started across the room, the door was opened and Thelma strode in. "What is it?" he demanded impatiently.

The housekeeper closed the door then stood regarding him sternly. "If you're planning to fire Emily because she let those children do a few chores, then you might as well fire me, too. It was my idea."

Jed's gaze traveled from one woman to the other. "I am not going to fire her," he growled. "But I want it understood that I don't want these children to feel they have to work for their living here."

"Making their beds and helping me put in a garden is not going to do them any harm," Emily replied in a reasoning voice, surprised by how calm she sounded under the angry intensity of his gaze.

His expression grew grimmer. "I don't want them to feel that they have to do it. I don't want them to think that their having a home here is conditional on their working for it."

Emily regarded him dubiously. "In other words, if they want to sit around all day and watch television, then I should let them do it."

"That's right." His jaw firmed even more. "They've been through a shock. They need time to feel secure again."

She understood how he felt, but her instincts told her he could be setting a bad precedent. However, he was the boss, she reminded herself. "Whatever you say," she conceded. As she turned toward the door she saw the worried look on Thelma's face and knew the housekeeper, too, was questioning the wisdom of Jed's decision. Emily turned back toward him, "But I think you're wrong."

The green of his eyes darkened in anger. "You'll do it my way."

Emily felt herself cowering under his glare. Then her back stiffened. No man was going to intimidate her! "They're good children right now," she said curtly, "but your attitude is going to turn them into spoiled brats. I knew their mother and she would have given them chores to teach them responsibility. *And* I can't believe you and your brother were allowed to lie around all day when you were growing up."

His jaw twitched with controlled fury. "This is different, and as you pointed out earlier, you are the hired help. That means you'll do as I say."

"You mind your manners, Jed Sawyer," Thelma snapped.

He recognized the housekeeper's presence with a quick glare before he returned his attention to Emily. "Do you understand my instructions?"

His gaze had narrowed threateningly and the urge to nod her head, back toward the door and make an escape was strong, but she forced herself to stand firm. Now that she'd begun, she was going to say what needed to be said. "I understand, but I still think you're wrong. The children have been through a terrible loss. Now it's your job to raise them to be responsible adults. You're not just their uncle any longer. You're their father."

Thelma added her two cents. "That's what I've been trying to tell him."

His gaze shifted from one female to the other. Frustration suddenly replaced the anger in his eyes. He raked a hand through his hair in an agitated manner. "I know and it scares the hell out of me." Turning away from them, he strode to the window and stood looking out.

The tiredness and worry that had suddenly been visible in his features before he turned away from her shook Emily. "I never pictured you as being scared of anything," she said quietly. It was the truth. She'd always thought of him as a man in total control of his world.

Turning back toward her, he regarded her dryly. "How would you feel if four children suddenly become your sole responsibility, especially when you've had as little experience as I have at fatherhood?"

"Scared," she replied.

Again his gaze shifted from one female to the other. As it came back to rest on Emily, he drew a terse breath. "All right. We'll try it your way for a while. But I don't want them to feel like slaves and I don't want them to think that their remaining here is contingent upon them doing chores."

"I'm not a slave driver and would never do anything to make them feel unwanted here," she assured him, stunned that he had actually backed down.

"Just make certain you don't." His voice carried a definite threat. Striding toward the door, he added grimly, "I've got work to do."

Before either woman could speak he was gone.

As the sound of his booted feet echoed down the hall, Thelma smiled at Emily. "I knew you'd be perfect for this job. He needed someone who could stand up to him and make him see the light."

"I feel more like I've been challenged to a duel," Emily muttered.

"Don't worry. He gets a bit gruff when he's worried. His bark's worse than his bite." Thelma headed out the door. "I've got to get back to the kitchen."

Left alone, Emily found herself recalling the frustration she'd seen on Jed's face and his admission that he was scared of the responsibility dropped so suddenly into his lap. He'd always struck her as the kind of man who would never confess to feeling any lack of confidence. But then she'd never pictured him as a family man, either.

Howard Parker suddenly came into her mind. For the children's sake she hoped that Jed had more staying power than Howard had.

Chapter Four

"**I**'m so glad you found a nice little niche for yourself." Mrs. Gyles greeted Emily with a warm smile. She was elderly and hard of hearing. Because of that she talked loudly and, as her voice carried across the crowded churchyard, Emily noticed several heads turn in their direction, then quickly turn away.

It was Sunday, and Emily had not been prepared for the interest that her arrival with Jed, the children and Thelma had stirred. She had hoped that word of her taking the job as nanny to the children had made the rounds and was already old news. But her hopes had gone unanswered. It must have been a slow week for gossip, she mused with a forced smile.

"You were always so good with children," Mrs. Gyles continued in motherly tones. But as her gaze shifted to Jed, she frowned worriedly. "However, I'm not so sure it's wise for you two to be sharing a house. You know how people talk."

"There is nothing for them to talk about," Emily replied firmly. She did know how people talked, and Mrs. Gyles was one of the busiest gossips in town.

Mrs. Gyles reached over and gave her hand a squeeze. "You know that and I know that but..." She let the sentence finish itself.

"Then we will have to count on you to assure people that there is nothing to gossip about," Jed interjected. Challenge flickered in his eyes. "You wouldn't want these children deprived of the care they need."

"No, no, of course not," Mrs. Gyles replied in flustered tones, clearly intimidated by the farmer.

"How's your arthritis?" Thelma asked quickly, changing the subject. "I hope the warmer weather has helped it a bit. Your daughter mentioned you had a bad winter."

Immediately Mrs. Gyles gladly launched into a discussion of her own health.

"I'm going to take the children down to their Sunday school classes," Emily informed Jed. She didn't want to wait around for someone else to pick up where Mrs. Gyles had left off. Her grip tightened on Amy's and Dennis's hands and she began leading them toward the side door of the church. "Linda and Drew, come along," she ordered over her shoulder.

She had expected Jed to remain behind, but he followed with the other two children. "Sorry about Mrs. Gyles," he said when they were out of earshot of anyone else. "With Thelma in the house as a chaperon I didn't think there'd be any talk."

What he meant was that he didn't think anyone would picture the two of them as a couple, she corrected mentally. The truth was she hadn't, either. Unexpectedly the image of him dressed only in his jeans flashed into her mind and a surge of heat rushed through her. *You're behaving absurdly,* she scolded herself. Aloud she said levelly, "I suppose it's only human nature to gossip, and I've survived worse."

"Gossip about what?" Linda asked, looking at Emily with wide-eyed interest.

"Nothing important," Emily replied with a note of finality, which said she wanted this discussion ended. They had reached the church basement where the rooms for Sunday school were located. "Which room do you go into?" she asked, determinedly changing the subject.

"Here, Mrs. Martin's class," Linda replied, coming to a halt in front of a door on their left.

"Good morning, Linda." Barbara Martin greeted the child with a bright smile, but her gaze was riveted on Emily standing in the doorway with Jed behind her. There was a definite question in her eyes.

"We'll pick you up for church," Jed called after Linda as she headed toward a group of her friends on the far side of the room.

The child waved back to indicate she had heard, then joined the other children.

Emily was already on her way down the hall toward Amy's room. She had thought that she would never allow gossip to bother her again, but the interest she and Jed were receiving was setting her nerves on edge.

"Don't you look pretty today!" Karen Lane greeted Amy with a honeyed smile as she came down the hall toward Emily, Jed and the children. Karen was a redhead in her midtwenties, with a lovely face and a figure that would entice any man. "And you boys look right handsome," she added.

Emily noticed that the smile on Karen's face didn't reach her eyes as the woman's gaze shifted from the children to Jed. Karen and Jed had dated on and off before he'd become the children's guardian. It was the opinion of the community that, if he should ever decide to marry, it would be either Karen or Josephine Crugger who would one day lead him down the aisle. But since the children had come under his care, he had curtailed his dating and was devoting all of his spare time to them.

"Morning," Jed said in an easy drawl, his smile charmingly crooked.

He had the look of a man whose interest had been aroused, and Emily experienced a sudden tightening in her stomach. She ordered herself to ignore it. It was merely a nervous reaction to all the attention she and Jed were receiving, she told herself.

"Morning," Karen replied, but her own smile still did not reach her eyes as her gaze shifted to Emily then back to Jed.

"Now that I have someone reliable to watch over the kids, I thought maybe you'd like to go out to dinner and a movie with me tonight," Jed said.

The smile reached Karen's eyes. "I'd love to," she cooed.

Jed grinned. "Pick you up around six."

"Six," she agreed and moved off down the hall, her hips swinging in a gently inviting rhythm. Over her shoulder, she added, "See you in Sunday school class."

Emily's limp suddenly seemed more pronounced to her than before. The thought of Jed watching her walk caused the tightening in her stomach to increase. "I'll get Amy settled. You take the boys to their rooms,'' she suggested to him.

He nodded and, passing her and Amy, led the boys to the far end of the hall.

I should be pleased about his date with Karen, she reasoned. *It will put a quick stop to the gossip. I am pleased,* she assured herself, ignoring the feeling in her stomach.

When she reached Amy's room, she discovered Helen Savory trying to keep track of nine two- to four-year-olds all by herself.

"Cheryl Avery was supposed to help this morning," the woman explained with a note of panic. "But she has the flu." She raked a wayward strand of gray hair from her face with her fingers. "And the children seem to be much more active today than usual."

Helen was in her late fifties and had been working with children this age for twenty years, but this morning she looked truly flustered. "I'll stay and help," Emily volunteered quickly. She told herself she wasn't hiding out—she was helping out. But she could not deny the relief she was feeling at not having to attend the adult Sunday school class with Jed and Karen.

Pushing them to the back of her mind, she concentrated on the children. But as the bell rang to announce the beginning of classes, the door of the room suddenly opened and Jed strode in with Karen tagging along behind.

"I was worried something might have happened to Amy when you didn't come up to class," he said, his gaze traveling around the room until he spotted his niece playing happily with another little girl.

"Helen was by herself," Emily explained quickly. "And there's a real mob here this morning, so I volunteered to stay."

"You see, I told you nothing was wrong," Karen purred, wrapping her arm through Jed's. Her mouth formed a pretty pout. "Now come on. We're already missing the beginning of class."

Jed shrugged and accompanied the redhead out of the room without protest.

"I do hope he's not going to start neglecting the children now that he has you to watch over them," Helen said worriedly.

Emily was having a difficult time trying to shake the strong dislike she'd experienced at the sight of Karen clinging to Jed. Firmly she told herself that this was due only to her concern for the children. As much for herself to hear as for Helen, she said evenly, "He does have his own life to lead. It wouldn't be natural for him to continue to devote all of his time to them."

"I suppose. It's not as if he asked to suddenly become a father to four children," Helen conceded. "And I can't fault his behavior so far."

"And speaking of children," Emily said, firmly changing the subject, "we had better devote our attention to the group here."

Helen cast a mildly disappointed glance toward the door through which Jed and Karen had departed, then with a motherly smile, she nodded her head.

By the time church was over, the news of the attention Jed was paying to Karen Lane had spread throughout the congregation, and any rumors about him and Emily had been squelched. As they drove back to his farm, she told herself she was relieved. But she didn't feel relieved. Again she told herself this was merely caused by a concern for the children. It would be hard on them if he began neglecting them.

"I have a few things over at my place I need to take care of," she said as they all sat around eating Sunday dinner. It was the truth, but she also wanted to put some distance between herself and Jed Sawyer. As hard as she tried to she couldn't stop the nagging little unpleasantness she experienced every time she glanced his way and pictured him with Karen Lane hanging on his arm.

"You run along," Jed replied. "I was planning to spend the afternoon with the kids."

A little later as she drove to her place, Emily ordered herself to put the farmer out of her mind. He was showing no signs of neglecting the children, and that was her only concern.

As she entered her home, her footsteps echoed on the hardwood floor of the entrance hall. The house seemed strangely quiet after Jed's house full of children.

She went into the kitchen and checked the refrigerator. She'd taken the perishables to Thelma, but she'd left the staples that would not spoil. "Just in case this job doesn't work out," she explained to the emptiness around her. She was already very attached to the children, but Jed Sawyer was another matter. There were times she would find him watching her as if she was some sort of curious specimen under a microscope. And although he seemed satisfied with her performance, she still wasn't so certain he wanted her around. "On the other hand, my being there has freed him to date Karen again," she muttered. This was meant to be encouraging because she did want to stay and take care of the children. But instead, the unpleasant little nagging returned. Determinedly she forced thoughts of her employer out of her mind and went upstairs.

She was in her bedroom boxing up some personal items she wanted to take back with her when she heard a car approaching. She walked over to the window and looked out. Every muscle in her body tensed as the vehicle pulled around the house and parked in the back. Watching the driver climb out, an acid smile played at one corner of her mouth. It was Howard, and he'd parked in the back so no one would know he was there. That seemed like an appropriate maneuver for the sneaky slime that he was.

They hadn't spoken since she'd been in the hospital. In fact he hadn't even had the decency to break their engagement in person. He had waited until the doctors had announced she would live but could be bound to a wheelchair or, at least on crutches for the rest of her life. Then he'd sent a dozen red roses with a letter explaining that he didn't feel they had a future together. Actually, she admitted grudgingly, in a way she owed him a certain amount of gratitude. She'd been deeply depressed by her parents' deaths, and even her engagement to Howard hadn't given her the kind of strength she needed to fight the doctor's predictions. The truth was she had been having her doubts about their engagement before the accident. But his callous rejection had spurred her pride and given her the anger and self-determination necessary to carry her through those painful days of therapy. She had been determined to walk again on her own and she did.

Hearing him knocking on the kitchen door, she considered ignoring him. They had nothing to say to one another. But her pride refused to allow her to hide like a cowering rabbit. Howard had no power to hurt her.

"I know I shouldn't be here," he said the moment she opened the door. "But I needed to see you."

Emily stood silently watching him. A hundred, maybe a million times, she'd thought about what she'd like to say to him if she ever found herself alone with him again. She had rehearsed telling him what a slime he was, what a snake. She resented him for making her the object of pity and ridicule. She knew that, although people had felt sorry for her when he dumped her, they had also been willing to understand his reluctance to take a crippled wife. She could understand that, too. What she resented was the fact that he hadn't had the courage to face her. She felt like a fool knowing that she had even considered marrying someone so weak. Now he was facing her and she was standing dumbly.

"I know you must hate me and you have every right to," he was saying. "I acted like a real heel."

Emily was surprised to hear him make this admission. Howard had never been one to admit he had behaved wrongly. But he owed this to her and she wasn't in the mood to let him off easily. "Yes, you did," she agreed.

"And I now know that I made a terrible mistake," he finished with a look of deep remorse.

Emily stared at him. His apology had given her a certain satisfaction, but she didn't like this last confession. She realized now that in the back of her mind she had been worried that, in spite of his behavior, she might still harbor some tender feelings for him. After all, at one point, she had consented to marry him. But all she felt toward him was disgust. His boyish charm had no effect on her.

He shook his head and his expression became even more mournful. "Mary has never understood me the way you did." He frowned with distaste. "And would you believe it, she's pregnant again!"

"I'm sure she didn't manage that on her own," Emily said.

He gave a disgruntled snort. "She was supposed to be on the pill but she forgot to take it."

Old memories sparked in Emily. It suddenly occurred to her that Howard had always found some way of blaming others for anything that went wrong in his life. "As you said, you really shouldn't be here," she said with dismissal.

But as she turned to go back upstairs, he caught her arm. "I have to stick it out with Mary until the baby is born, but then I'm leaving her. I'd like to think there is a chance for us."

He was trying to crawl back to her! There had been vengeful moments when she'd imagined this happening. But now that it actually was, she felt sick to her stomach. "What you should be thinking about is Mary and your children." When the going got rough, Howard's response was to get going, she mused. He was like a child who refused to accept any responsibilities. She suddenly found herself thinking of Jed Sawyer. Jed might be a little rough around the edges, but he was a man a person could depend upon. The children were very lucky to have him. With a glare of disgust, she attempted to jerk free from Howard's hold.

Anger showed in his eyes, then it was quickly replaced with a pleading look as he captured her other arm and held her pinned in front of him. "I know you loved me once. You can learn to love me again."

"I apologize if I'm interrupting anything."

Howard's face paled. He released Emily so abruptly she lost her balance and stumbled backward. She fought to keep her footing, but it was a losing battle. Letting out a small shriek, she began to fall. Suddenly two large callused hands closed around her waist from behind and steadied her. Glancing over her shoulder, she found herself looking into a pair of icy green eyes.

"Thelma thought you might need help loading up whatever it was you came over here to get," Jed said coolly.

"I'd better be going," Howard muttered, backing toward the door. In the next instant he was gone.

Making certain Emily was steady, Jed released her as if he found touching her distasteful. "Sorry I barged in. Didn't know you were having a rendezvous," he said in a voice that held more accusation than apology.

Her jaw tightened defensively. Jed was obviously ready to believe the worst of her. "I wasn't having a rendezvous! Howard's appearance here was a total surprise to me."

He continued to regard her frostily. "He should have been home with his wife and kids."

"I agree," she replied, adding with self-righteous indignation, "and that's what I told him."

But he didn't look convinced. "Fooling around with a married man usually only leads to trouble," he warned.

"I'm not planning to fool around with a married man," she snapped. His cool gaze was unnerving her.

With an impatient scowl she demanded curtly, "Can you honestly picture me as a femme fatale luring a man away from his wife and children?"

Almost immediately she regretted her words. A sudden silence fell over the room as Jed's gaze began to travel slowly over her. He started with her hair, then turned his attention to her neck and downward to the mounds of her breasts softly outlined by the fall of her shirt.

Emily had experienced male inspection before, but it had never felt like this. Her body warmed beneath his gaze and her blood flowed faster. It was as if he could see beyond her covering of clothes, and she flushed with embarrassment as his inspection moved to her abdomen and hips. Mentally she pictured her scars. No man would find them enticing. An icy chill cooled her blood. But it heated again as he continued to follow the lines of her body in an unrushed fashion. His gaze was like a physical touch as it traveled down her legs, causing them to feel curiously weak. Her breath quickened and her tongue came out to wet her suddenly dry lips.

When his eyes reached her toes, he began to retrace his inspection as if he wanted to be certain he hadn't missed anything. As his gaze again reached her face, she forced herself to meet it levelly. What he thought of her feminine appeal or lack of it didn't matter, she told herself tersely. But the coolness in his eyes caused a hard knot in her stomach, and unconsciously her top teeth fastened on her bottom lip to keep her chin from trembling. Obviously he agreed that she was no threat to any man's marriage. It was what she had expected. Still, the feeling of rejection that spread through her was stingingly sharp.

"Don't sell yourself short. You've got enough of the right attributes to turn a man's head," he growled, abruptly breaking the heavy stillness between them. Turning away from her, he headed toward the door. "I'll be waiting on the front porch. Let me know when you want me to carry any boxes for you."

Emily stared at his departing back. Listening to his steps as they echoed down the hall toward the front door, his words played through her mind. He hadn't found her unattractive. He'd actually decided that she could be a threat to a man's marriage. A pleased excitement stirred within her. Then she scowled at herself. "You're acting as if your ladder is missing a top rung," she scolded herself under her breath. Jed Sawyer wasn't interested in her as a woman. He was interested in Karen Lane. Not only that, he thought that she could stoop so low as to be considering breaking up Howard's marriage!

She gave her shoulders a sharp shrug and, forcing her legs into motion, walked toward the front of the house.

Jed was standing, leaning against one of the pillars holding up the porch roof. His arms were crossed in front of him and his expression was grim, as if he preferred to be any place else but there.

"I don't need any help," she said with dismissal. "I'm sure I can manage on my own."

The frown on his face deepened with impatience. "As long as I'm here, I might as well make myself useful."

Emily started to insist that he leave. But the words died in her throat. He might think she was hoping Howard would be waiting to return when he saw Jed's truck pull out. "Fine," she said, and with a shrug to indicate that she didn't care if he stayed or left, she went back into the house.

She had returned to her bedroom and was adding some books to one of the boxes she wanted to take with her to Jed's when she heard his step on the stairs. She glanced up as Jed reached the door of her room and came to a halt.

A surprised expression played across his face as his gaze traveled around the room taking in the white lace curtains, the pink bedspread and the matching ruffled pink canopy that arched over her bed. "Never pictured you surrounded by pink and lace," he muttered.

His admission that he considered her out of place in this very feminine bedroom caused her back to stiffen with pride. "I suppose you think a woman has to be all giggly and silly and seductively flirtatious to be the type who likes any sort of feminine decor."

"Guess I did sort of think they went hand in hand," he admitted with a dry smile. Abruptly his expression became strictly businesslike. "If that box is full, I'll carry it downstairs."

"It's full," she replied, grateful for any excuse to be rid of him. Again she found herself hurt by the fact that he didn't consider her very feminine. Considering that she was living under his roof, she should be happy with his attitude, she told herself. But instead it grated on her nerves. Quickly she stepped back to avoid any contact as he approached and picked up the box. "I've been spending too much time on my own," she muttered to herself as he descended the stairs and she was once again alone in her room. These reactions she was having to him were totally irrational. What he thought of her was unimportant.

Still, when he returned she could not shake off the unsettling effect his presence in her bedroom caused. He seemed to fill the empty space, and she was acutely aware of him watching her. She felt clumsy and almost dropped a porcelain music box.

In one long stride, he crossed the distance between them and helped her catch it as it tumbled around in her grasp. His large callused hands felt hot as they brushed against hers, and waves of heat shot through her.

Her eyes locked on the music box. Her body was behaving like a foolish schoolgirl's, and she was afraid he would read her reaction on her face. He would probably be shocked and then amused, she guessed. He'd made it perfectly clear she wasn't his type of woman.

Furious with herself for this irrational physical attraction she was having toward the man, she secured the music box and, stepping away from him, quickly packed it. "That's everything," she announced brusquely. The need to escape this close confinement with him was strong.

Her nerves were just on edge because of Howard's showing up unexpectedly and then Jed's arriving and accusing her of considering breaking up Howard's marriage, she reasoned as she followed Jed back to his place. By the time they reached the house, she was certain she had her body under control and the rational side of her mind once again in command.

But later that night, she found herself tossing and turning, unable to sleep. Jed was out with Karen, and every time Emily closed her eyes she found herself picturing them together. "Who he is with and what he is doing is none of my business," she muttered as if hearing herself speak the words could make them so. But her restlessness refused to go away. Finally giving in to it, she pulled on her robe and quietly made her way downstairs. Not wanting to disturb Thelma, she went into the den and switched on the television. Flipping through the channels, she found an old science-fiction movie. It was one of the really dumb ones with obvious artificial scenery and costumes left over from a Hercules movie. "Perfect," she murmured, snuggling down into the cushions of the couch. It had been movies just like this that had helped her make it through those first long lonely nights right after she'd left the hospital.

"Emily."

Emily curled up tighter trying to ignore the male voice that threatened to interrupt her sleep.

"Emily, wake up," the voice coaxed softly.

A large hand was gently shaking her shoulder. She forced one eye to open. The final credits for the movie were running across the screen. Groggily, she opened the other eye and looked up. Jed Sawyer was standing behind the couch looking down at her, his expression shuttered. Mentally cursing herself for falling asleep and letting him find her down here, she shifted into a sitting position.

"No one has waited up for me since I turned eighteen," Jed was saying in a dry teasing tone.

Emily glanced over her shoulder momentarily to glare up at him. She couldn't let him think he had anything to do with her being there. "I wasn't waiting up for you. I was having trouble sleeping—ouch!" She'd turned her head back and a muscle had pulled in her neck.

Two strong hands began to massage her shoulders and neck. "If I'd known you were going to be this grouchy, I'd have tried carrying you up to your bed without waking you," he muttered, the teasing quality gone from his voice. "But I thought maybe something had happened with the kids and you wanted to talk to me about it."

"The kids are fine." She marveled that she had been able to speak coherently. Heat was radiating through her. The way he was gently kneading her shoulders and neck made her want to purr. Even more disturbing was the thought of him carrying her up the stairs. From the top of her head to the tips of her toes, her whole body was aware of his touch. *This is crazy!* she screamed to herself. *To him you're about as appealing as a lump of clay.*

Jerking free from his touch, she rose to her feet. She wanted to make a run for the door but pride held her back. Picking up the remote control, she switched off the television. "I'll be going upstairs now," she said tightly, adding over her shoulder as she forced herself to move with casual dignity, "Good night."

"Good night, Emily," he responded to her back.

She didn't turn around. She could still feel his touch on her shoulders, and the lingering heat it caused was making her toes want to curl.

She heard him behind her as he turned off the lights and followed her up the stairs. The sudden thought of the two of them going to the same room caused a rush of excitement to prickle her skin. *You are crazy!* she chided herself as she reached the door of her room and heard him going into his.

She entered the room and closed the door, then stood staring at her image in the mirror. "So I'm attracted to him," she confessed aloud. "It's a natural reaction. He's a relatively good-looking man, certainly a virile one, and I'm not dead." Her jaw tensed. "But it's not going any further than this. In the first place, he doesn't find me appealing and even if he did, I'm not ready to settle for a one-night stand or even a prolonged affair, and that's all he'd be willing to offer." Having had this little talk with herself, she tossed off her robe, turned off the light and climbed into bed. But as she closed her eyes, she saw his image and found herself wondering how it would have felt to be carried upstairs by him.

"Thoughts like that will only lead to trouble," she muttered.

The problem, she decided, was that she'd kept to herself for too long. The reactions she was having toward Jed were too acute to be real. They were born out of nervousness. That was the answer—she was overly tense, strung out. Any day now she would begin to relax and this disturbing effect he was having on her would fade.

Chapter Five

It didn't fade.

During the next month she found herself dealing with a muddle of emotions. That Jed wasn't dating Karen Lane exclusively pleased her. She told herself this was because she didn't think Karen was the right person to fill the role of mother to the children.

He also didn't date as frequently as she had expected him to. Instead he devoted most of his evenings to his nieces and nephews.

But when he did go out, she would find herself restlessly pacing about the house.

This has to stop, she told herself firmly one evening as she stood in the doorway of the den. He was watching television with the children and she found herself wishing she could be sitting beside him. She was behaving like a high-school girl having her first crush. Musingly she thought of Howard. Even when she'd been fooled by his charm into thinking she was in love with him, he'd never made her feel this way. She gave her body a quick shake and, turning away, started up the stairs. This attraction wasn't rational, and there was certainly no future in it. Somehow she had to get rid of it.

The ringing of the phone stopped her halfway up the stairs. But before she could retrace her steps back to the hall, Drew had rushed out and answered it. She was about to continue up the stairs when he suddenly extended the receiver toward her. "It's a man and he wants to talk to you," he announced.

As she took the receiver and said hello, Emily felt a prickling on the back of her neck. Glancing over her shoulder she saw Jed watching her with an unreadable expression. Abruptly he turned his attention back to the children.

"Emily, this is Tom Miller," a male voice was saying over the line.

Mentally she pictured her caller—he was her age, about five foot ten, brown hair, brown eyes, pleasant features, divorced. He was part owner of the largest car dealership in town and, since his divorce, a confirmed bachelor. They had dated a couple of times in high school but there had never been anything serious between them.

"I was wondering if you would like to go out to dinner this Friday night," he said.

Her first reaction was to refuse. Then she frowned at herself. Tom was pleasant company and she'd been thinking she needed a diversion to take her mind off of Jed. Starting to date again could very well be the answer. "I'd love to," she said, adding hesitantly, "But I'll have to check to see if I can get the night off." Friday was supposed to be one of her two official nights off, but she hadn't taken it since she'd started working, and she wasn't certain Jed hadn't made plans.

"What night do you want off?"

She jumped at the sound of the male voice so close behind her. Whirling around, she saw Jed leaning against the doorjamb of the living room only a few feet away. The children were clustered around him, watching her expectantly. "Friday," she replied.

"Your Friday nights are your own," he replied with a shrug. Then he strode back into the living room. The children followed.

"Friday is fine," she said into the receiver. Tom made arrangements to pick her up at six and she said goodbye and hung up. *A date will do me good,* she told herself firmly as she started back up the stairs.

"Emily."

Startled, she turned to find Jed at the bottom of the stairs.

He was studying her with an impatient frown. "I was wondering if I could have a few words in private with you." It was more of an order than a request.

"You're not going to get married and leave us, are you?" Linda demanded from behind her uncle.

"I wasn't planning on it," Emily assured her.

Jed's impatient frown deepened. "Go back in the living room and watch television," he ordered.

Linda glanced worriedly up at Emily, then obeyed.

Wondering what she had done to cause Jed to be angry with her, Emily followed him into his study.

"After I found you and Howard at your place a few weeks ago, I figured he'd be leaving Mary soon," he said when the door was closed and he was satisfied they were alone. He regarded her with a fatherly reproving expression. "I know it's none of my business, but do you think it's smart for the two of you to start dating so openly so quickly?"

Emily stared at him. He thought it had been Howard on the phone. "In the first place, you're right," she said levelly, "it isn't any of your business. In the second—"

"Actually it is my business," he interrupted. "There's bound to be a lot of nasty gossip and I don't want my nieces and nephews caught up in it."

"In the second place," she began again in clipped tones, "that was not Howard on the phone. I tried to tell you at my place that I have no intention of having anything to do with Howard. He's a married man and Mary is welcome to him. If you must know, it was Tom Miller on the phone."

He continued to regard her narrowly. "Never thought of you as Tom's type."

She shrugged. "Maybe he's decided to change his ways."

"Or yours," Jed suggested in a warning voice. "Maybe you should reconsider this date."

He was treating her like a kid sister. Frustration welled inside of her. "*You* are giving *me* advice about who to date? You, who choose to date the likes of Karen Lane and Josephine Crugger?" Abruptly she closed her mouth tightly as he raised a questioning eyebrow. She had come very close to sounding jealous. Her shoulders straightened with pride. "I'm willing to overlook your taste in women and you can ignore my taste in men," she finished with polished dignity then, her limp barely perceptible, she strode out of the room.

Friday came, and Emily took special pains to look her best as she dressed for the evening. She felt as nervous as a schoolgirl. It had been a long time since she'd been out on a date. She choose a white eyelet dress with a fitted bodice and a full skirt. She didn't feel steady in high heels but she had a pair of white sandals with sensible heels that looked quite dressy. She gathered her hair loosely with a red ribbon so that it flowed in waves down her back, and she carefully applied a little makeup to her eyes and lips.

"You look great!" Drew said approvingly when she came downstairs. The other children echoed his sentiments.

"Don't you think she looks great?" Linda suddenly demanded of Jed as he came out of the living room to join the inspection team.

Again Emily experienced a disquieting sensation as his gaze traveled over her. What really bothered her, however, was how interested she was in his answer.

"She looks fine," he conceded.

But the polite smile on his face didn't reach his eyes, and she caught the underlying disapproval in his voice. Well, Tom Miller wouldn't have been her first choice for a date, either, but lately he was the only one who had asked. Her theory was that once she started dating, someone more acceptable would come along. Besides, what right did Jed have to disapprove of her actions, she asked herself acidly as a knock sounded on the screened door. In the next moment, Karen Lane entered.

She was wearing a low-cut kelly-green sundress with matching four-inch heels that clicked rhythmically on the hardwood floor as she walked toward them, her hips swinging gently and seductively. The girls watched her dubiously, but Emily noticed that there was fascination on the boys' faces as Karen approached. Men, she thought, attempting to ignore the sudden rush of jealousy that swept over her.

Karen was carrying a bakery box. Beaming at the children, she said a gushing hello as she slipped a possessive arm around Jed's waist and gave him a quick kiss on the cheek. "Since you've been so kind as to invite me to dinner, I thought I'd bring the dessert," she said, looking up at Jed with a sensual smile that implied she had a special dessert in mind just for him. Returning her gaze to the children, she dangled the box by its string toward Drew. "Would you mind taking this in to Thelma and tell her that it has to be refrigerated?"

Like a slave ready to obey her every command, he accepted the box as if it were a gift of gold and hurried toward the kitchen.

Karen's attention now turned to Emily. "Well, don't you look..." She paused in her inspection of Emily as if finding the right word was proving a bit difficult, then finished in a honey-coated patronizing tone, "sweet."

Emily smiled wryly. "And you look..." she began, then stopped herself. She wasn't going to participate in a cat fight and most certainly not in front of Jed. She tossed him a how-dare-you-criticize-my-choice-of-dates glance, then smiled politely at Karen. "Lovely," she finished.

Karen looked surprised, then shrugged as if the compliment was deserved and gave Jed her full attention.

"I think Emily looks lovely," Linda suddenly interjected pointedly, frowning up at her uncle.

"They both look lovely," Jed conceded with a patronizing smile.

Feeling like one of the ugly sisters the prince was being kind to, Emily said, "Now that that's settled, I think I'll wait for my date on the porch." And before anything else could be said, she went outside.

Inside she heard Karen turning on her charm and telling the girls how pretty they looked. If flattery could win friends, by the end of the evening, Karen would be an adopted member of the family. *It doesn't matter,* Emily told herself firmly. *I'm not in competition with her.* Still, her nerves were already on edge by the time Tom showed up.

The date didn't start off badly. He gave a pleased wolf whistle when he saw her, which buoyed her spirits, and he offered his arm in a very gentlemanly fashion. And he did drive her all the way into Columbia to take her to a really nice restaurant. But during the salad he began to make casually subtle remarks about them both being adults. By dessert he was suggesting that they go back to his place and watch a couple of movies on his VCR. "Kick off our shoes, relax and see what happens," he finished with what Emily guessed was supposed to be a seductive smile but looked more like a leer.

She had politely refused this suggestion, and he had made a few snide remarks about deserving something for taking her to such a nice place. She had ended the date by insisting on paying for her own dinner and having him drive her directly home.

It was barely ten when they turned into the drive leading up to Jed's house. Emily made a silent plea that the children would already be in bed and Jed and Karen wouldn't take any notice of her arrival. To her surprise she noticed that Karen's car was gone. But to her chagrin, she saw Jed sitting on the front-porch swing.

Tom pulled up and stopped the car long enough for her to get out. Seeing Jed on the porch, he yelled out sarcastically, "Guess you won't have to use your air conditioners much this summer with Emily around." Then, gunning his engine, he turned in the circular drive and drove off.

"Men!" Emily muttered angrily as she climbed the porch steps.

"I don't think I like being thrown in the same category as Tom Miller," Jed commented, rising from the swing.

"Fine, you can have a category all your own," she replied dryly. As she spoke, it occurred to her that he *did* belong in a category all his own. *But it's a category where I don't fit in,* she reminded herself.

"Thanks, I think." Coming to a halt in front of the door, he blocked her way and studied her narrowly. "You all right?"

"I'm fine," she assured him, except for a strong case of embarrassment, she added to herself, wishing he would just let her pass without any more conversation.

"I warned you Tom wasn't your type," he pointed out, continuing to block her escape into the house.

"Okay, you were right," she conceded tightly.

"I'd suggest that in future, you choose your dates with a little greater care," he continued in a reprimanding manner a father might use with an impetuous child.

Emily's embarrassment turned to anger. He had a lot of nerve talking to her about her choice of dates.

Here was a man with four children to raise, and he spent his time with a female who didn't have a domestic bone in her body. She bit back a suggestion that he might consider taking his own advice. Obviously a woman's domestic side wasn't what interested him. But she was suddenly curious as to why he was alone. The children were obviously in bed. Surely Karen would have wanted to be here now. Glancing around as if just then noticing that the redhead was missing, she said with a practiced nonchalance, "By the way, what happened to your date?"

Jed shrugged one shoulder. "That dessert she brought was one of those fancy cakes with some sort of liquor or brandy in it. I didn't notice until everyone had a piece in front of them. Figured it probably wouldn't hurt, so I let the kids eat it."

Emily glared up at him, her own disastrous date forgotten. "You let them eat it?" Her eyes rounded as the full implication of what he was saying sank in. "You let Amy eat it? She's only three!"

"I learned my lesson," he assured her with a scowl. "Amy got sick and threw up. She was sitting on Karen's lap at the time. Karen was a little upset and went home. But I have to admit the kids are all sleeping real peacefully."

"Serves her right," Emily muttered, picturing the redhead with a sick child in her lap. "What idiot would bring a brandied cake for young children to eat!" Her eyes flashed in fury. "And what idiot would let them eat it? They'll probably have hangovers tomorrow. I've got half a mind to take the day off and leave them to you."

A crooked smile played at one corner of his mouth. "And I'd deserve it," he admitted. His gaze softened and, reaching out, he traced the line of her jaw. "You remind me of a she-cat protecting her young."

His touch left a trail of fire. Startled by the intensity of it, she looked up into his eyes only to find herself being drawn into their green depths like a swimmer caught in a whirlpool. Her anger vanished as her breath locked in her lungs. The urge to reach out and test the feel of his jaw was so strong her hand began to move upward.

A flicker of surprise showed in his eyes. "Emily?" he said her name in a slow questioning drawl.

You're making a fool of yourself! her inner voice screamed at her. Drawing a quick shaky breath, she jerked her gaze away from his and took a step back out of his reach.

His eyes narrowed with purpose. Moving toward her, he caught her chin and forced her to look up at him.

But she'd spent a great deal of time since the accident promising herself that no man was going to make a fool of her again. "Don't," she ordered warningly, again jerking free from his touch.

"You don't have to be afraid of me," he said impatiently.

It wasn't him that she was afraid of. It was her weakness for him that frightened her. "I just think it would be better if we kept a distance between us," she said tightly.

"Are you sure that's what you want?" he challenged, tracing the line of her jaw.

Her whole body flamed, but she forced herself to consider reality. He was probably feeling frustrated, since his date with Karen had ended so abruptly. If she gave in, all she would be was a convenient female to satisfy his male urges. Another thought brought an icy chill. When he saw her scars he'd probably lose all interest, and that would make her humiliation complete. Her control now firmly back in place, she met his gaze with frosty determination. "If you want me to stay and look after the children, you'll keep your distance."

For a moment challenge again flickered in his eyes, then he shrugged. "If that's the way you want it, my little ice maiden, that's the way it'll be." Stepping aside, he held the door open for her.

Her shoulders stiff with pride, she went inside.

The next morning, Emily steeled herself to face him. All night, dreams of him had taunted her and she wondered if he would keep his word to keep his distance. If he didn't she would have to leave. Her ability to resist him was irrationally weak.

He greeted her at breakfast in the polite but cool manner he had been greeting her every day since her arrival. *Obviously having someone to take care of the children is more important to him than adding another notch to his bedpost,* she decided. She told herself she was glad. She'd grown very fond of the children and she wanted to stay and take care of them.

"We didn't mean to make Karen angry," Linda said, breaking the unusual silence at the breakfast table.

Jed gave her a friendly smile and a wink. "It's all right. No harm done."

Linda didn't look convinced. "She was real angry." Her cheeks flushed. "She even said you weren't any fun any longer."

"I'm sure she'll change her mind about not seeing you again if you send her some flowers," Drew suggested encouragingly.

Emily glanced worriedly toward Jed. When he said Karen had gotten a little upset, she hadn't realized how serious it had been. But he didn't seem concerned.

"Don't worry," Jed assured him. "I'll take care of it."

But that afternoon, it was Emily who received flowers. The dozen pink roses came with a card that read:

I apologize for my boorish behavior. It will never happen again.

Jed

"Who are they from?" Thelma demanded as Emily read the card.

"I owed Emily an apology." Jed answered for her as he entered the kitchen just at that moment. It was obvious he had been working in the barn when the delivery van had arrived. His clothes were dusty and he smelled of hay. Taking off his Stetson, he wiped the stream of sweat from his brow with his sleeve, leaving a streak of mud. Watching Emily with a shuttered expression, he added, "I hope she'll accept it."

He was letting her know that he meant to hold to his promise to keep his distance. Again she told herself she was glad and ignored the hard little knot that formed in her abdomen. "Your apology is accepted," she replied levelly.

Thelma's gaze traveled from one to the other. "You two want to tell me what this is all about?" she asked encouragingly.

"No," came the reply in unison. Immediately Jed turned and left the house while Emily took the flowers and a vase up to her room. But as she put the pink blooms in water she found herself wondering if Karen was at this moment arranging a dozen roses of her own. Probably, she decided. And most likely, Karen's note asked for a date that evening.

But to Emily's surprise, Jed didn't go out that night, and when Karen came up to speak to him at church on Sunday he was cool toward her.

As usual during the week, he worked from dawn until after dark. When he came in, he ate, played with the children and went to bed when they did. And he kept his word about maintaining a distance between himself and Emily. He spoke to her only when it was necessary and only in the most businesslike manner.

On Wednesday he informed her that he would be going out Saturday night. She'd heard that Karen had started dating Brian Davies and wondered who Jed was going to be taking out. There were several possibilities. None of which was any of her business, she told herself.

But on Saturday night as she sat on the porch watching him drive away, an emptiness suddenly filled her. *You're being ridiculous,* she chided herself. The house was full with her and Thelma and the children. She was glad he was gone. She even told herself she hoped he had a good time.

"I was sure surprised by Jed's choice of date tonight," Thelma said, interrupting Emily's thoughts.

Coming out onto the porch, she stood watching the cloud of dust left by Jed's car.

Emily told herself she wasn't interested, but she heard herself saying, "Really?" in a questioning voice.

Thelma turned to study her narrowly. "He's going out with Cheryl Avery."

Emily couldn't hide her surprise. Cheryl Avery was a pleasant-looking woman, a couple of years younger than Emily. But Emily would never have pictured Jed with her. Cheryl was quiet, a bit on the shy side and most definitely an old-fashioned female who had her mind set on marriage and a family. "Maybe he decided he should try dating women who were safer to have around the children," she remarked dryly.

"Or maybe he's decided that those children need a mother and he's looking for someone suitable," Thelma suggested. "It's my opinion that if that's the case, he should look a little closer to home. If you fixed yourself up a bit, you'd be right appealing, and I can't think of anyone who'd suit the children better."

Emily flushed. Fixing herself up wouldn't do any good. Once she'd told Jed to keep his distance, he'd complied without any protest. No, he found her about as interesting as an old shoe. "I think I'll just stay the way I am," she replied with an air of indifference. "I was never any good at putting on a false front."

Thelma sighed. "I've always liked you. Thought you and Jed might learn to like each other real well once you got to know each other. Looks like I was wrong."

About one of us, Emily corrected mentally. Aloud she said, "I'd better go check on the children."

All evening she tried not to think about Jed, but as she lay in bed later that night, she tossed restlessly. She told herself it wasn't him that bothered her. If he married she would have to leave, and she would miss the children.

A headache began to build. Climbing out of bed, she found some aspirin and went downstairs for a glass of water. She was in the kitchen when she heard Jed's car pull in.

Scowling, she glanced down at herself. The weather had turned warm. Planning only a quick trip and not expecting to encounter any other member of the household, she had come down barefooted and wearing only a nightgown and a hastily pulled on lightweight cotton robe. As she lifted her head she caught a glimpse of her reflection in the kitchen window. Her hair was in wild disarray and even in the dim image she could discern the tired circles under her eyes. Saying a silent prayer that Jed would go directly upstairs, she fastened her robe just in case and combed her fingers through her hair in the hope of putting it into some sort of order.

Neither her hope of making herself more presentable nor her prayers were answered. She heard his footsteps coming toward the kitchen. Quickly swallowing the aspirin, she started toward the door but it was too late.

"Evening," he said, entering the room.

Chapter Six

Emily considered making a dash for the door but that would look cowardly. "Evening," she replied.

He came to a halt only a couple of steps inside the kitchen. She would have to skirt close by him to get out. "Did you have a nice time?" she asked, trying to ignore the tantalizing effect his after-shave was having on her senses. The minute the words were out, she wished she had bitten her tongue. She didn't want to know if he'd enjoyed himself, and she most certainly didn't want him to think she cared one way or another.

Frowning musingly, he leaned against the door, blocking her exit. "Have you ever made a chocolate soufflé?"

Startled by the question, Emily blinked. "What?"

Shoving his hands into the pockets of his slacks, he continued to stare grimly at the cabinets beyond her.

"Spent a whole hour listening to Cheryl explain to me about how to make a chocolate soufflé."

Emily read the impatience on his face. Clearly he'd been bored. He'd probably spent the entire evening comparing Cheryl's conversation to Karen's mindless but entertaining banter. Suddenly picturing herself in Cheryl's shoes, she said, "You probably made her nervous and she couldn't think of anything else to talk about."

"I suppose," he conceded. His gaze narrowed on Emily. "What would you have talked about?"

There was a challenge in his eyes as if he was comparing her with Cheryl and wondered if women of their type could talk about anything that interested him. Think, she ordered herself. But instead, the intensity of his gaze only made her more aware of her disheveled appearance. How she looked didn't matter to him, she reminded herself curtly. Even when she looked her best, he considered her about as femininely alluring as a piece of furniture. "I don't know," she replied levelly, wanting only to escape.

The frown on his face deepened. "You must have some sort of topic you make small talk with."

His insistence surprised her. Suddenly it dawned on her that he was using her to find some sort of line of conversation to liven up his next date with Cheryl, and her stomach knotted. It wasn't her job to coach him for his dates! "I'm not very good at small talk," she replied stiffly. "Now, if you don't mind moving, I'd like to go back to bed."

A smile tilted one corner of his mouth and the green of his eyes darkened with amusement as he continued to lean against the door. "That's a much more modern line than I would have imagined you using."

Emily glared at him in frustration, then frowned when she realized the way he had twisted her words. All she wanted was to escape and he was teasing her. "That wasn't a line," she snapped.

He scowled impatiently. "Can't you take a joke?"

Her cheeks reddened as she realized what a prudish spinster she sounded like. Nervously she raked a hand through her hair. "I didn't mean to sound so uptight. It's just that I have a headache and I'm not in the mood for bantering," she said in calmer tones.

He was studying her again, this time with an intensity that caused a prickling on the back of her neck. "You must have something you say when a dead silence threatens," he persisted. "What would you have talked to me about?"

She was too tense to think, but it was obvious he wasn't going to let her leave without an answer. "I don't know. I would probably have been too busy wondering why you had asked me out and not someone who was more your type." Her teeth closed over her bottom lip as she realized what she'd said. She'd practically asked him why he had dated Cheryl.

He continued to regard her grimly. "And if I told you I had decided that I needed a wife who would be a good mother to my children, what would you say?"

Emily felt nauseous. Hearing him confirm Thelma's suspicions was harder than she had thought it would be. "I don't know what Cheryl would say," she said stiffly. "I suppose you will have to have this conversation with her." Frantic to escape she added curtly, "I really do have a splitting headache. Would you please get out of my way?"

He hesitated for a moment longer then, straightening away from the door, he opened it and allowed her to pass.

Upstairs in her bed, she again told herself it was only because she would miss the children that this new information made her feel so terrible. She tried to find consolation by telling herself that Cheryl would make them a good mother. But instead, she found herself picking out all of Cheryl's weak points. Finally giving in to exhaustion, she dozed.

The next morning she wished she'd used her headache to skip church. She'd offered to help with the toddlers because Amy seemed to like it when she was around. But she hadn't expected to be paired with Cheryl Avery.

"Helen is under the weather today," Cheryl explained, glancing beyond Emily expectantly, then breathing a sigh of relief when she realized that Emily and Amy had arrived alone. Waiting until Amy had wandered off to join the other children, she turned her attention back to Emily. "I don't know how you manage to live under the same roof with Jed Sawyer. He made me a nervous wreck last night." She held up her hand in a sign of peace. "I don't mean to imply that he was anything other than a gentleman," she assured Emily. "I just don't know exactly what it was. He just made me nervous."

Cheryl had always struck her as the jittery type, Emily thought, again finding herself willing to focus on the other woman's weaker points. The temptation to paint Jed as overbearing suddenly looked strong. But she couldn't do that. "He's not so difficult to get along with once you get to know him. You were probably overly nervous because it was your first date with him."

"I suppose," Cheryl conceded. She gave a small shrug. "But he intimidates me. I don't know if I want to go out with him again if he asks." There was a hint of a question in her voice as if she expected some advice from Emily.

Emily ordered herself to say something encouraging. Cheryl was certainly much better for the children than Karen. But the words stuck in her throat. Jed hadn't hired her as a matchmaker, and if he wanted Cheryl Avery he was going to have to get her himself. "I'm sure you'll make the right decision," she said diplomatically.

"He is quite a hunk," Cheryl admitted, a sudden gleam sparking in her eyes. Then it was replaced by anxiety. "But I'm just not sure he's good husband material. And," Cheryl added with a thoughtful frown, "I'm not so certain I want to take on four children who aren't even mine."

Emily had a tremendous urge to call Cheryl a fool, but instead she said evenly, "Speaking of children, I think it's time we devoted our attention to the ones in here."

Cheryl was forced to follow as Emily crossed the room. It took some doing, but Emily managed to avoid any further personal conversations with the woman for the rest of the morning.

Later as she rode home in the back seat of Jed's car, she wondered if he was going to grill her that afternoon about what Cheryl had said to her. She'd never liked being in the middle of romances, and she especially didn't want to be in the middle of this one. She had Sunday afternoon off, and she decided that before Cheryl's name could be mentioned she would go over to her place and spend the time dusting and getting it into order. She hadn't been able to get herself to rent it. This job with Jed Sawyer felt too uncertain, and she wanted a place to go to if it should suddenly come to an end.

But to Emily's discomfort, Thelma wasn't as anxious to avoid the subject of Cheryl Avery as Emily was. The housekeeper was riding in the front seat with Drew and Jed. Looking over the boy's head, she said bluntly to Jed, "I was wondering if I should be setting an extra plate at the table this evening for Cheryl."

"Nope," Jed replied in an easy drawl.

"You planning to go out tonight then?" she persisted, adding innocently, "I just want to know how many places to set."

Unconsciously Emily's hands balled into fists as she braced herself for the news that he was going to ask Cheryl out again. She guessed that the woman would accept. Cheryl might not be enthusiastic about the children and she was intimidated by Jed, but the gleam in her eye said she was still interested.

"I'm not going out tonight," he answered, adding with a frown, "I don't like women who look at me as if I'm the big bad wolf who's going to pounce on them at any moment."

So Cheryl wasn't going to get the opportunity to decide. Emily glanced at the back of his neck and wondered if he'd given up the idea of finding a suitable wife. Apparently Thelma had the same thought.

"Suppose this means you'll be dating Karen again. Provided you can pry her off Brian Davies," the housekeeper muttered. "You just better warn her not to bring any more of those cakes over."

"I don't think I'll be seeing her again, either," Jed replied with a nonchalant shrug.

"You could always ask Emily for a date," Linda suggested hopefully.

Jed glanced in the rearview mirror at Emily's reflection. "Emily and I have an understanding," he said dryly. "We stay ten paces from each other at all times."

He was politely but firmly discounting her from his list. Emily's chin suddenly threatened to tremble. Angry with herself for this weakness, her teeth closed on the inside of her bottom lip as she fought to maintain a facade of indifference. *You already knew that was how he felt,* she chided herself. *And it's fine by me,* she added. *I want something more from a marriage than what he's willing to offer.*

Thelma gave a short snort of disapproval but said nothing.

When they reached Jed's place, Emily helped Amy change into play clothes then, going into the kitchen, she informed Thelma that she wasn't going to stay for the large noon meal. Instead, she made herself a sandwich to take with her and left.

Feeling in need of some company, she also took Harrington. "Just like old times, huh, boy?" she said as she parked in front of her house and climbed out of the car. But it didn't feel like old times. The place felt cold and hollow, and a restlessness and sense of aloneness haunted her.

Passing the hall mirror, she stopped and frowned at the image reflected back at her. If Jed was looking for a wife, maybe she should fix herself up a bit. Then she scowled at the wistfulness that had appeared on the face in the mirror. He hadn't given her a second glance since she'd ordered him to stay away from her. Obviously he felt no attraction toward her.

"And what I've been feeling for him is just a silly schoolgirl infatuation, anyway. It'll go away soon," she told herself sternly. "I need to start looking around for someone to date."

While she cleaned she went over the list of available males. None of them interested her. She kept finding herself comparing them to Jed. He wasn't the handsomest of the lot, but the way his eyes sparkled when he was amused caused a warm tingle to run along her spine. And he was so surprisingly gentle and understanding with the children. Then there was the way he looked in the middle of the night in a pair of hastily pulled on jeans without his shirt or boots, his hair rumpled—

"Stop it!" she ordered herself harshly. "Forget about him!"

"I hope that isn't me you're so angry with."

Emily whirled around at the sound of the familiar male voice. Howard was standing in her kitchen doorway. He was the last person she wanted to see. "What are you doing here?" she demanded.

"I was out for a drive and saw your car," he replied in an easy drawl, ignoring the anger in her voice. A boyishly pleading look came over his features. "Had to get away from all the screaming and crying at home."

Recalling the last time Howard had stopped by, she glanced nervously over her shoulder, half expecting Jed to suddenly appear. "You shouldn't be here."

Howard smiled slyly. "If you're worried about us being interrupted, don't be. Car phones can come in real handy. Jed's out on a wild-goose chase at the moment."

Emily shook her head. Howard never considered the inconvenience he caused others simply to have his way. "You should be home with Mary helping her. She looked especially tired in church today."

He rewarded this suggestion with a shrug of indifference. "She's the one who keeps getting pregnant."

Emily glowered at him. How could she ever have thought she was in love with a man who was so shallow? "She isn't doing it all by herself."

"She's the one who keeps forgetting to take her pills." He gave another shrug as if to say that the subject of his wife bored him. "I heard you went out with Tom Miller. You really should be more selective. Obviously Jed Sawyer has been a bad influence on you."

Emily regarded him icily. "What I do and who I see are none of your business."

Approaching her, he cupped her chin in his hand. "You used to be so sweet and innocent." A smile suddenly lightened his expression. "But I have to admit, I find you more interesting this way."

His touch was causing a cold creeping sensation on her skin. "Go home," she ordered, taking a step away from him.

Challenge flickered in his eyes. "I know you're angry with me and you have a right to be. But you don't mean that."

Emily glared at him. He honestly thought she could still be attracted to him. Harrington wandered in at that moment and, seeing Howard, gave a low growl. The dog had never liked Howard. She'd have to consider Harrington's taste more seriously from now on, she decided. Aloud she said, "Leave now or I'll sic Harrington on you."

A momentary flash of fear showed on Howard's face, then vanished as he smiled boyishly. "All right, I'll leave for now. But I'll be back."

Before she realized what he was going to do, he had again captured her chin and, tilting her face upward, placed a light kiss on her lips. The contact left her cold.

Poor Mary, she mused as she watched him driving away. But then, the woman had been willing to go after Howard while Emily was lying crippled in a hospital bed dealing with her parents' deaths and the possibility she might never walk again. Maybe Mary had gotten what she deserved. "Still, I owe her a debt of gratitude," Emily said, patting Harrington on the head.

She had finished the cleaning and was wondering how she was going to spend the evening when the phone rang.

"I'm worried," Thelma said the moment Emily said hello. "Jed got a call nearly three hours ago saying the bull he keeps pinned in the north meadow had gotten loose. He took the Jeep and went out there and hasn't come back since."

So that had been Howard's ploy, Emily realized. But Thelma was right. Jed should have been back. Howard would never have actually turned the bull loose. He was city bred and didn't like walking across fields or getting near animals. "I'll come back and go check on him," she said, hanging up without even saying goodbye.

When she pulled up at the house, the children and Thelma were gathered on the porch waiting. Leaving the others, Drew ran toward her, his young face filled with anxiety. "Shouldn't Uncle Jed have been back by now?"

"He probably got stuck in the mud someplace," she said soothingly, hiding her own worry. Even if he'd gotten stuck, he could have walked back by now. "Or maybe he found some bit of fence that needed immediate repairing. It probably wouldn't occur to him that anyone here would worry about him," she added for her own encouragement, as well as the children's and Thelma's. "I'll take the truck and go see what he's up to."

Drew started toward the vehicle. "I'll come with you."

Apprehension swept through Emily. If Jed was injured, it might be best if the child wasn't with her when she found him. "I need you to stay here with Thelma and help her keep an eye on your brother and sisters," she insisted. Adding with a reassuring smile, "Besides, when I find your uncle I plan to give him a piece of my mind for worrying all of you, and I don't want you to hear it."

Drew didn't look convinced. "But if he's hurt, you'll need my help."

Thelma had followed Drew and now took his hand. "You let Emily get going," she ordered gently.

"Take your brother and sisters inside and play a game with them," Emily added. "I'm counting on you to keep them from worrying too much."

Drew looked disgruntled but nodded in agreement.

Glad the truck had four-wheel drive, Emily drove toward the north meadow. She had to force herself to go slowly over the rough terrain. Each time she had to stop to open a fence, her nerves grew more tense. She prayed Jed hadn't had an accident, that he had simply found a chore that needed taking care of. After all, he was used to his time being his own. Of course if that was the case, she had a few choice words for him.

She was skirting a newly plowed field when she spotted him sitting on a boulder. The Jeep was nowhere in sight. Coming to a halt, she drew a shaky breath. So he had just gotten stuck. He'd probably never thought about anyone worrying about him and had spent all this time trying to get unstuck before he decided it was impossible without help and had started to walk back to the house.

"Do you have any idea how worried the children and Thelma are about you?" she demanded, climbing out of the truck and walking toward him.

Lifting his head, he scowled at her. "Keep your voice down. I've got one hell of a headache."

Emily's breath locked in her lungs. There was a trickle of dried blood on his cheek. Approaching him, she lifted his Stetson from his head.

"Ouch!" he gasped.

Emily's chin trembled when she saw the blood-matted hair on the left side of his head. "What happened?"

"A doe ran out in front of me. I swerved to miss her and went into a damn gully. The Jeep turned over and I got thrown out," he explained tersely. "I got dizzy trying to walk back so I sat down to rest awhile."

He could have been killed! She wanted to wrap her arms around him, but that would probably shock him more than the spill from the Jeep. "Come on," she said shakily, taking hold of his arm, "I need to get you to a hospital."

"Don't need any hospital," he growled through clenched teeth as he rose to his feet. "I just need to get home."

She felt something wet and sticky as she slipped her arm around him to give him more support. Looking at his back, she had to fight to keep from gasping. His shirt was torn and blood soaked.

"You need to go to the hospital," she insisted, as they moved slowly toward the truck.

"Don't need to go to any hospital," he growled again. "Thelma can call Doc Wilson. He'll come over and patch me up."

Her hold on him tightened protectively. "You're the most stubborn man I've ever known."

They had reached the truck and with her help he managed to climb inside.

She tried to drive carefully but it wasn't easy over the uneven terrain. Each time the truck was jarred, she saw the taut lines of pain deepen in his face and her stomach knotted more tightly. Thelma and the children came out as she neared the house.

"I'm only stopping for a minute to tell them that you're going to be fine, then I'm taking you to the hospital," Emily said, shifting the truck into park but leaving the engine running.

Jed's hand closed around her wrist. "I'm not going to any hospital." There was a thin white line of pain around his lips. "It's another hour down the road and I couldn't take your driving for that long."

Emily was frantic with worry, and her temper flared. "There's nothing wrong with my driving. And we weren't on a road. We will be when we go to the hospital."

He closed his eyes as if he was having trouble concentrating. "I need to lie down."

Before she could argue further, he had opened his door and was climbing out of the cab. Quickly switching off the engine, she jumped out of her side and hurried around to his. By the time she reached him so had Thelma and the children.

"You've been hurt," Drew was saying, looking pale and shaken.

"Just need a few stitches from the doctor and I'll be fine," Jed replied with a reassuring smile.

Thelma glanced toward Emily questioningly. "He refuses to let me take him to the hospital," she said with an angry scowl.

Jed tossed her a hostile glance and saw the flash of pain the movement of his head cost him. Turning to Thelma, he ordered, "Call Doc Wilson." Looking down at the children, he winked and smiled. "You all run along and play."

"Go along," Emily seconded the order when the children didn't obey. "I'll take care of your uncle." For their sake she added, "He just needs a little rest."

"Come along." Thelma shooed the children in front of her like a mother hen with her chicks. "I need to get inside and call the doctor."

As the others moved away, Emily turned toward Jed. He was leaning against the truck. To the casual observer it looked as if he was merely lazy but she knew he was doing it for support. "Okay, cowboy," she said. "Come on. I'll help you inside. But I still think you should go to the hospital."

"It's just a bump on the head," he muttered. "I've had worse."

"Was it all those blows to your head that made you as stubborn as a Missouri mule, or were you just born that way?" she asked, slipping an arm around his waist and easing herself under his arm so she could function as a human crutch.

"I don't see any reason to go to a hospital when they'll just put me in a bed and make me lie there for two or three days. I can rest easier in my own bed," he growled back.

He was very unsteady and her fear for him grew. "If the doctor says you need to go to the hospital, I'm going to get you there if I have to hog-tie you."

A crooked smile tilted one corner of his mouth. "You would too, wouldn't you?"

"Damn right," she said through clenched teeth.

"The doc's on his way," Thelma said as they passed through the hall and started up the stairs. Spotting the children watching from the doorway of the den, she shooed at them with her hands. "You kids go on and play," she ordered. "Emily will take care of your uncle."

But their faces grew pale as they saw Jed's back.

"It looks worse than it is," Emily told them. "Remember how Dennis's leg looked when he scraped it?" she added to give credence to her words.

They nodded. There had been a lot of blood and Dennis's jeans had been ruined, but the leg had healed quickly. "Emily and the doctor will get Uncle Jed well," Drew said with authority, then ushered his brother and sisters back into the den.

Emily wished she had the child's confidence as she helped Jed into his room and sat him on the bed. He didn't even have the strength to take off his hat.

Gently she eased it from his head. His eyes were closed and she saw the lids tighten as if her simple act had multiplied the pain a hundredfold. Shifting her attention to his feet, she removed his boots and then his socks.

"I need to lie down," he muttered.

As he eased himself over to lie on his stomach, she helped by lifting his legs. At least he didn't seem to have any broken bones. Howard suddenly flashed into her mind and deep anger swept over her. He never cared who he hurt just as long as he got what he wanted. How could she have been so blind? Because she was young and innocent and he was very good at hiding his true self, she justified. Still, the next time she saw him, she planned to give him a piece of her mind.

"I'm going to take off your shirt and clean up your head and back," she informed Jed. She had to see how bad his wounds really were. The buttons were under him and she didn't have the heart to try to turn him on his side. The shirt was ruined anyway. "I'll be right back."

"I'm not going anyplace," he assured her.

Quickly she found a pair of scissors. She returned to his bedside and carefully began cutting the shirt and peeling it away from the wound. As she worked, her gaze shifted from his back to the half of his face she could see. His eyes were closed and his jaw was tense with pain. A jab of pain shot through her and she realized that his pain seemed to be her pain.

By the time she had peeled away the last of the cloth, his breathing had become shallow. The skin was badly scraped and it looked as if there was one, maybe two gashes deep enough to require stitches. But it was the head wound that frightened Emily. Suddenly she became fearful that he had lost consciousness. "I should have taken him to the hospital," she muttered, furious with herself for giving in to his demand to come up here to his room.

"I don't need to be in any hospital," he growled back. "How's it look?"

She breathed a shaky sigh of relief. At least he was still conscious. "Like you lost," she replied.

A brisk knock suddenly sounded on the door. In the next moment, Thelma entered with a handful of washcloths and a pan to hold water. "Thought you might be needing these," she said, approaching the bed. She looked at Jed worriedly. "How bad is it?"

"The back should mend," Emily replied, relieved to have a third party in the room. "It's the head injury that worries me."

Thelma placed an arm around Emily's waist and gave her an encouraging hug. "He's got a head like a rock."

"Emily compared me to a mule," Jed muttered. "The least one of you could do is to say something sympathetic instead of insulting."

"He's going to be just fine," Thelma announced with a nod.

But the knot stayed in Emily's stomach. "I'll start cleaning him up," she said, taking the basin from Thelma. She filled it with warm water from the bathroom and returned to his bedside, then began to gently wash his back.

"The ride to the hospital might have been easier than your ministrations," he grumbled, sucking in a gasp of pain.

"Men are never easy to be around when they're sick or injured," Thelma observed knowingly. Handing Emily a towel and the rest of the washcloths, she added, "There's no sense in both of us being exposed to his tantrums. I'll go wait for the doctor. You can take care of the patient."

Emily felt a powerful urge to stroke Jed's jaw gently and murmur soothing words in his ear. Glancing at the departing housekeeper, Emily was tempted to ask Thelma to cleanse the wounds and let her go wait for the doctor. But a stronger part of her refused to turn Jed's care over to anyone else. Left alone with Jed once again, Emily shifted her attention to the head wound. The back could wait; she had to see how badly his head had been injured.

He let out a low groan as she began to work, then clamped his lips together tightly and lay quietly. To her relief the cleansing caused only a little fresh bleeding, but the size of the lump scared her. If she could have gotten her hands on Howard just then, she would have strangled him.

She had the head wound decently cleaned and was halfway finished with the back wound when the doctor showed up. Shooing her out of the room, he took over.

Emily breathed a sigh of relief as she stepped out into the hall. Her body ached from the strain of her fear for Jed.

Going downstairs, she found the children outside, huddled together on the front porch swing, waiting. They all looked up at her expectantly. "He's going to be all right, isn't he?'' Drew asked, assuming his usual role as spokesperson for the group.

"He's going to be fine," she replied. But the children continued to look anxious. She couldn't blame them. They'd just lost their parents. They had to be terrified of losing Jed, too.

And head wounds could be unpredictable. A fresh wave of panic swept over her. It wouldn't do for the children to guess how frightened she was. "I'm going to go back upstairs in case the doctor needs to give me instructions," she said with forced cheerfulness. "Why don't you all play catch?" she added over her shoulder as if there was no reason for them to worry. But as the screen door swung closed behind her, she glanced back and saw they hadn't moved.

Upstairs in the hall, she paced for what seemed like forever before Doc Wilson came out of the bedroom.

"He should go to the hospital," he informed her. "But I've never won an argument with Jed yet." He shook his head, then his gaze narrowed on her. "I'm going to count on you to take care of him."

Chapter Seven

"**M**e?" Emily balked. She was having a hard enough time controlling her emotions without being put in charge of Jed's health.

"You'll have Thelma to help you," the doctor continued. "But when Jed sets his mind to something, he can make her back down. I'm counting on you not to give in. He has to stay in bed until I'm satisfied he's all right. That will be for at least three days. I've told him this, but telling him and making him do it are two different things. I had to stitch him up in a couple of spots and I gave him a tetanus shot and left some antibiotics for him to take. The instructions are on the bottle. Start them in six hours. But it's the head wound that worries me. Someone has to stay with him at all times for the next forty-eight hours. If he gets nauseous, I want you to call me immediately. And," his tone became even more commanding, "he has to be woken every hour. Talk to him. Ask him his name. If he's coherent, fine. If he's not, call me.''

As the doctor headed for the stairs, he added over his shoulder, ''I'll tell Thelma what I've told you.''

''Doc,'' Emily called out after him.

Pausing, he looked back at her.

''He is going to be all right, isn't he?'' she asked around the lump in her throat.

''You just follow my instructions,'' he replied with a fatherly smile. ''I'll be back tomorrow to change the dressings.''

It was a noncommittal response and a chill ran along Emily's spine. Promising herself that she would follow the doctor's orders to the letter, she drew a steadying breath and entered Jed's room. To her relief, she found him already in bed. Obviously the doctor had helped him finish undressing and had tucked him in.

Jed was lying on his stomach. A sheet had been pulled up to his waist and a large bandage covered the major portion of his back. The head wound had been left uncovered. He opened one eye to see who had come into the room, then closed it. ''I just need to sleep,'' he said groggily. ''You go take care of the kids.''

''Considering your current attitude, I'd rather do that,'' she lied. Wild horses couldn't have dragged her away from him, but she wasn't going to let him know that. ''However, the doctor has left orders that someone is supposed to stay with you at all times, and for the moment, that's me.''

''That's not necessary,'' he growled.

It hurt that he was trying to get rid of her. ''Fine. You can always go to the hospital,'' she retorted.

Clamping his mouth shut, he said no more.

Maybe this was for the best, she reasoned, attempting to find a bright side to the accident. By the time Jed was cured of his wounds she was certain to be cured of her infatuation.

Thelma came up a few minutes later and they worked out a schedule. For the rest of the afternoon and evening they took turns watching over Jed and waking him. But as night fell, Emily could see the tired circles under Thelma's eyes.

"I'll take the whole night shift," Emily volunteered when they had finished tucking the children into bed. "I can sleep sitting in a chair."

"Are you sure?" Thelma asked, but there was relief on her face. With a sigh she added, "I am feeling tired. It's been a long day."

"I'm sure," Emily assured her. The truth was, as rotten as Jed had acted, she wanted to be the one to watch over him. *You're an idiot,* she told herself as she settled for the night in the large overstuffed arm chair that occupied the corner of the room nearest the window.

It was a very masculine room with a large four-postered bed. Clearly it had been the master bedroom when his parents were alive. But now it showed no signs of any feminine habitation.

On the bureau was a picture of Jed's parents taken on the day of their wedding. Restless, Emily rose and picked it up for a closer inspection. They were a handsome couple. Like her, Jed had been born and raised here in Randolph's Well, Missouri. She knew his history. His mother had died in childbirth when he was fifteen. The baby had died, too. His dad had had cancer and passed away when Jed was in his early twenties. Jed had always liked farming, but his younger brother, Bill, hadn't. Jed had seen that Bill went to college. Bill had become an accountant, and when their father died, sold his share of the farm to Jed.

Emily sighed and, setting the picture back down, approached the bed. "Okay, grouchy," she muttered under her breath. "Time to wake up." In louder but gentle tones, she said, "Jed?"

"I'm Jed Sawyer and I want to sleep in peace," he growled back at her. "If I wanted someone waking me up at all hours of the day and night, I'd have gone to the hospital."

"Well, at least you're coherent," she muttered back.

Straightening, she stood beside the bed looking down at his long form, half-covered by the sheet. She owed Doc Wilson a debt of gratitude. He'd had a talk with the children on his way out and had assured them that their uncle would be fine as long as he got some peace and quiet. After that they had tiptoed around the house and in general behaved like paragons.

A breeze stirred the curtains. Now that the sun had set, the air was a bit cooler. Reaching down, she gently covered Jed up to his shoulders with the sheet.

A sudden smile played at the corners of her mouth. She had learned something else about Jed Sawyer today that had surprised her. He was shy.

It had been early evening and she had been taking her turn watching over him. He'd opened one eye and said in a commanding tone, "Get Thelma."

Putting aside the book she'd been unsuccessfully trying to read, she'd looked at him. "Thelma is fixing supper. What do you want?"

His jaw tensed. "I want Thelma."

It hurt to think he disliked having her aid. "I can get you anything you want."

An embarrassed flush darkened his cheeks. "I need to use the bathroom and I don't own a pair of pajamas and I don't have the strength to pull on a pair of jeans. Now go get Thelma."

The thought of seeing him in nothing more than the pair of briefs he was wearing under the sheet had caused a stirring of interest that shocked her. "I never thought of you as being bashful in front of a woman," she said with an edge of amusement.

His jaw tensed more firmly. "Emily." He said her name threateningly.

For a moment she had considered insisting that he let her help him. She was physically stronger than Thelma. But her weakness for him scared her. She could still feel the lingering imprint of his body from when he had leaned on her so that she could get him into the house. "I'll go get Thelma," she said.

But she'd stayed outside the door just in case Thelma needed help.

Jed's gruff voice brought her back to the present. "Is there something you want?"

Realizing she was still standing looking down at him, she scowled at herself. "No." Feeling the need to offer an explanation, she added, "I was just trying to decide if you were already asleep."

"I have a hard time sleeping when people are staring at me," he replied impatiently.

"Sorry," she muttered. Feeling like a nuisance, she returned to her chair. *At this rate, at least by morning, I should be cured of any infatuation,* she told herself.

A gruff male voice interrupted her thoughts. "I'm the one who should be apologizing."

Startled, she glanced toward the bed to find Jed watching her.

"I've always been a royal pain when I'm sick," he continued sheepishly. "Thelma usually keeps her distance whenever possible."

"I can understand why," she replied, shaken by his apology. It would have been easier to deal with her feelings if he'd continued to remain querulous.

A small smile tilted the side of his mouth that she could see, and closing his eyes, he dozed.

As the night wore on and she grew too tired to stay awake, she set the alarm on the clock to wake her every hour so that she could rouse Jed.

The first time it went off, he greeted the sound with a groan of pain. "What . . . ?" he demanded.

"I was afraid I would doze off and miss waking you," she explained, quickly turning off the ringing.

He grumbled under his breath, but didn't say anything discernible.

She knew the noise must have caused his head to ache even more. But she'd set the sound down as far as it would go and she did need it to wake her. "I'm sorry," she apologized. "But I'm only following doctor's orders."

"It's all right," he mumbled back.

He was certainly behaving more civilly, she mused as she reset the alarm. It gave her hope that he was feeling better.

The sun was breaking over the horizon when she shifted in the chair and a sharp shooting pain in her neck woke her. Groaning softly, she eased herself into a more upright position. Her gaze immediately went to the bed. Jed had freed one leg from the sheet and she found herself fascinated by how strong and sturdy it looked. Men are supposed to ogle women's legs, she admonished herself. Women aren't supposed to ogle men's. But it was a very masculine leg.

"Morning," Jed said gruffly.

Embarrassment reddened her cheeks as her gaze swung to his face to find him watching her. Then the embarrassment turned to puzzlement followed by panic as she realized it was morning. She looked at the clock and gasped. "We've been asleep for five hours!"

"Would you please keep your voice down," he requested. "My head still feels like a marching band is practicing maneuvers there."

"Why didn't you warn me this clock was unreliable?" she demanded accusingly. Picking up the offending piece of machinery, she frowned at the alarm switch. It was turned off. "I know I set this," she muttered.

"I waited until you were asleep, then turned it off," he confessed. "Now can you stop talking about that damn clock and get me some aspirin for my head?"

She glared at him. "You turned it off? You could have lapsed into a coma. And it's half an hour past the time for your antibiotic."

"Emily," he said through clenched teeth, "I told you my head is killing me. I'm in no mood to listen to you throw a tantrum."

"Me throw a tantrum? I'm not the one who's behaving childishly," she snapped, fighting back the panic caused by thoughts of what could have happened.

"I could use some peace and quiet," he growled.

Clamping her mouth shut, she got him a glass of water and his medication.

"What about the aspirin?" he asked, looking down at the antibiotic.

"You can't have any yet," she replied.

He groaned as he levered himself up on an elbow to take the pill. "Feels like every muscle in my body is sore," he grumbled. "Ouch," he gasped as he lay back down.

"What happened?" she demanded, her panic rising at the intensity of the pain in his voice.

He drew a terse breath. "My shoulder muscle just knotted."

Immediately setting aside the glass, she found the knotted muscle and began to massage it.

"You have a nice touch," he murmured as the muscle began to relax.

The firm feel of him beneath her palms caused a warmth to spread through her. The temptation to kiss the spot where the offending muscle had knotted was like a delicious agony. *Get away from him,* she ordered herself.

"Don't stop," he pleaded gruffly, when she started back toward her chair. "That's the first time I haven't ached all over since that Jeep threw me."

She knew it was dangerous, but she couldn't deny him. Returning to his bedside, she began to massage his shoulders and neck.

"Did you know you snore?" he asked in a lazy drawl as she worked her way along his arm then back to his neck.

"If you're trying to flatter me so I'll keep this up, that's not the way to do it," she warned, and her cheeks reddened at the thought of herself sounding like a buzz saw.

"It's not an offensive snore." He smiled crookedly. "Just every once in a while you give this little snort."

She suddenly found herself wondering if Karen or Josephine snored. Most likely they didn't sleep in his company, she reminded herself. The thought caused a cold lump in her abdomen, and she was overcome by a desperate need to escape. "I'm going to go down and see if Thelma has the coffee brewing," she said stiffly, and without a backward glance she fled the room.

Out in the hall, she came to an abrupt halt and stood rigidly, her hands balled into fists at her sides. Even after his ill-humored behavior and his teasing, she was still attracted to him. He wasn't that impossible, her little voice pointed out. He was in a lot of pain. He had a right to be grumpy. Besides, he did apologize once. *I can't believe it! I'm making excuses for him,* she wailed mentally. She shook herself as if that would get rid of the jumble of emotions within her. It didn't.

She took a deep breath. He wasn't interested in her as anything more than a nanny for his children, she reminded herself curtly. Feeling suddenly very tired, she went down to the kitchen.

During the remainder of the day, she and Thelma took turns watching over Jed. He slept most of the time. But by late afternoon he showed signs of getting bored. The children had been anxious to visit him to see for themselves that he was going to be all right. Emily decided they could entertain him and allowed them in.

Linda read him every Dr. Seuss book she owned, and Emily marveled at his patience as he lay there listening. When Linda was finished, Drew offered to play checkers with him, but Jed said he wasn't ready for that yet. They settled for bringing in the television and the children sat quietly watching while Jed dozed.

The doctor came soon after dinner. After examining his patient, he said that Jed was progressing well, but he wanted him to stay in bed for another couple of days.

"I've got a farm to run," Jed protested, trying not to grimace from the pain as he shifted himself into a sitting position.

"Emily knows what to do," Doc Wilson replied matter-of-factly. Turning to Emily, he told her without compromise, "Keep him in bed." Then he left.

The expression on Jed's face worried her, but he didn't make any further protests. He simply lay back down and went back to sleep.

That night Emily again slept in the chair in Jed's room.

"I hired you to play mother hen to the children, not me," he said when she came in with her pillow and began to settle in for the night.

That he seemed so anxious to be rid of her hurt. "And I'd gladly leave you on your own, but Doc Wilson made me promise I would keep an eye on you for one more night," she informed him coolly.

His expression became one of grudging acceptance. "Then you might as well be comfortable. You can have the other half of the bed."

As Emily's gaze traveled over the large empty portion of the bed, the thought of lying beside him sent a wave of excitement coursing through her. Idiot, she berated herself. She might as well be a stick of furniture as far as he was concerned. Still, she was too old-fashioned to accept the arrangement. "I don't think that's such a good idea," she said.

He scowled impatiently. "You'd be perfectly safe. I'm in no mood or shape to try to molest any female."

And even if he was, it wouldn't be her, she added to herself. The thought stung. "I was thinking that I would probably toss around and jar the bed," she said in level reasoning tones as if she had never considered the possibility of anything physical between them. "That wouldn't help your headache or your soreness."

For a moment he looked as if he was going to argue with her, then he gave a shrug, winced when it caused him pain, closed his eyes and went back to sleep.

While Jed slept peacefully, Emily slept restlessly. By morning she was exhausted and gladly relinquished her guard over the patient to Thelma and the children.

When she'd come to work for Jed, he'd arranged for her to hire Hank Johnson to look after her place. Yesterday she'd called Hank and asked him if he could also help her with the chores at Jed's place while Jed was laid up. Hank had agreed. She was in the barn, checking with the hired hand to make certain everything that needed to be done was getting done, when Drew came running out shouting for her.

Panic that Jed had fallen and injured himself further swept over her, and she started back toward the house at a trot with Hank close behind her.

"Uncle Jed's up and getting dressed," the child gasped out, meeting her halfway.

Coming to an abrupt halt, Emily took a steadying breath. "I can take care of this," she informed Hank, her panic replaced by anger. Drew looked terrified and her heart was still pounding violently. Jed had no right to upset everyone this way!

She rushed to the house and climbed the stairs two at a time. In the hall upstairs, she found Thelma and the rest of the children all gathered outside Jed's door.

"He ordered us out and locked the door," Thelma said as Emily reached her. "I knew I shouldn't leave him but he got that set to his jaw he gets when he's going to have his way no matter what."

"He might die," Linda said between tiny sobs. "You've got to stop him, Emily."

Kneeling, Emily gave the young girl a hug. Over Linda's shoulder she saw Linda's fear reflected in Amy's and Dennis's faces. "He's not going to die. He's too hardheaded for that," she said reassuringly. Her face became etched with determination. "But I am going to see that he follows the doctor's instructions." Straightening, she went over to the bedroom door and pounded on it. "Jed Sawyer, open this door immediately," she ordered.

"Stop that banging," came a growl from inside. "I've got a headache."

"You *are* a headache!" she shouted back and pounded on the door again.

"All right, all right." His voice sounded closer to the door. It was followed by a click.

"Take the children and go downstairs and have some breakfast," Emily ordered Thelma. "I'll take care of this cowboy."

"If he gets past you, we'll block the exits," Thelma promised. The children all nodded in agreement.

As they started down the stairs, Emily entered Jed's room and closed the door behind her. She had a few choice things she was considering saying to him and she didn't want an audience.

He had on his jeans and shirt and was sitting on the side of his bed, pulling on a pair of socks.

"The doctor said you were to stay in bed today," she said, approaching him and standing in front of him. Anger flared in her eyes. "On top of that, you've got the children scared half out of their minds."

"I'm sorry about the kids, but I'm fine and I've got work to do," he replied matter-of-factly. "I've never coddled myself and I don't intend to start now."

She heard the pain in his voice and her fear for him grew. "My mother used to say that most men don't have any sense when it comes to taking care of themselves. I suppose it has something to do with that macho image you have of yourselves. Nothing is going to keep you down. Well, you're wrong! I am." The determination on her face grew. "I've got Hank Johnson doing your chores and I'll check on things during the day." Kneeling in front of him, she pulled off the socks he had just put on.

"Dammit, Emily," he snarled. "Putting those things on wasn't easy. My head feels like it's going to split open when I bend down." Rising to his feet, he pointed toward the door. "Get out of here and let me dress."

Rising, too, she stood facing him. "I will not leave until you promise me you'll go back to bed."

He glared down at her. "I told you, I've got work to do. I'll take a nap this afternoon."

She could see the pain lines etching themselves even deeper into his rugged features. "I was wrong," she snapped as her concern for him grew even stronger. "You're not as stubborn as a mule—you're twice as stubborn." She knew what she had to do. Stiffly, she began to unbutton his shirt. "But I can be just as stubborn. You're going back to bed."

He caught her wrists. "As much as I would enjoy standing here and letting you undress me, I have work to do."

There was a gruff suggestive edge to his voice that caused a hot curling sensation deep within her. She told herself he was only mocking her. Still, the heat of his hands as he held her captive traveled up her arm and the pulse in her throat began to throb. A sudden questioning look came into his eyes and she quickly lowered her gaze. She couldn't let him guess how much he affected her. It would only embarrass them both. "The least you could do is think about the children. They're terrified something is going to happen to you," she admonished, working her hands free. Applying herself to unfastening his shirt, she added, "They've been through too much already."

"Maybe you've got a point," he conceded, standing rigidly while she finished with the last button.

Surprised by his sudden surrender, she could feel him watching her but she didn't dare look up. She'd never thought that taking off a man's shirt could seem so intimate. *He's your patient, nothing more,* she told herself. But that didn't stop her heart from pounding harder.

He suddenly swayed forward and she was forced to press her hands against his chest to steady him. The feel of the hard musculature and crisp curly hairs beneath her palms caused her knees to weaken. *You're behaving like a schoolgirl with her first crush,* she chided herself. Aloud she said tersely, "You can't even stand without help."

"I guess I'm not quite as steady as I thought I was," he admitted, sinking back into a sitting position on the bed. Looking into her face, a challenge flickered in his eyes. Reaching up, he traced the line of her jaw with his fingertips, then followed the taut cord of her neck to where the pulse throbbed. "And you're not as immune to me as you want me to believe."

She felt like a fool. She knew she should have pulled away from his touch immediately, but it had been too intoxicating. She closed her teeth over her bottom lip to keep her chin from trembling. Forcing her legs to move, she took a step back, breaking the contact. "You're not stupid," she said. "You know you're an attractive man. And while I'm not interested in becoming another notch on your bedpost, I'm not made of ice, either." Suddenly realizing the admission she had made, she flushed with embarrassment. Why hadn't she kept her mouth shut! She had to get out of there before he started laughing. Heading toward the door, she didn't look back as she added curtly, "I'll send Thelma in to make certain you get back to bed."

Thelma and the children were waiting at the bottom of the stairs. "Jed is going back to bed," she informed them evenly. To Thelma she added, "Would you please go see if he needs any help? I'm going back outside to finish my business with Hank." The truth was she had to get out of the house. At any moment she expected to hear a roar of laughter from upstairs.

As she headed for the barn, the flush on her face deepened. "Notch on your bedpost," she muttered under her breath. How could she have said such a thing? *Because I'm tired and he unnerves me,* she defended. As she reached the barn, she glanced back toward the house. *Just forget you said it,* she ordered herself. *I'm sure Jed will get a good laugh out of it, then put it out of his mind.*

When she returned to the house, Thelma met her in the hall to tell her that Jed had gone back to bed and the children were up there keeping an eye on him. Glancing at her watch, Emily realized it was time for his medication, but her legs refused to carry her upstairs. She wasn't ready to face him yet and the amusement she was certain would be in his eyes. "Would you mind checking on him and making certain he takes his medication?" she requested. "I'll straighten the den." When the housekeeper looked at her questioningly, Emily added, "I need a break. He can be a very trying patient."

"Most men are," the housekeeper replied, heading toward the stairs.

Emily had finished running the vacuum when a car pulled up outside. To Emily's surprise, it was Vivian Cramer.

"I've come to see how Jed is," the woman said, when Emily came out onto the front porch to greet her. Vivian was in her late fifties but looked much younger. Her husband was a banker and she'd lived a much easier life than that of a farmer's wife. She was dressed stylishly in a tweed suit and high-heeled shoes and was carrying two large prettily wrapped packages.

"I'll tell him you're here," Emily said, opening the door and guiding the woman toward the living room.

"I really don't want to disturb him," Vivian said laying a restraining hand on Emily's arm. She smiled a motherly smile. "Actually I was hoping to see my granddaughters."

Between her embarrassing encounter with Jed and her lack of sleep, Emily's patience was wearing thin. "What about your grandsons?" she asked. She knew she shouldn't have said anything, but she couldn't help herself. She couldn't understand how a grandparent could only care for some of their grandchildren and not all of them, especially when the boys were so nice.

"Them, too, of course," Vivian conceded, but her smile looked forced. Breathing a sigh, she added, "The truth is I think of them more as Sawyers and the girls more as Cramers." She shook her head. "My daughter could have married so much better."

"She married just fine."

Emily looked up the stairs to find Jed coming down. "You shouldn't be up," she said, her embarrassment over their earlier encounter overshadowed by her sudden anxiety. She quickly started up the stairs toward him.

"I'm fine," he assured her, his attention remaining on Vivian.

"I didn't mean to come here and upset you," Vivian said, watching him dubiously as if she thought he might turn into a raving beast at any moment. "I simply thought maybe you would like for me to take the girls home with me for a few days while you finish recovering."

"Emily can watch over them just fine," Jed said, stopping halfway down the stairs.

Moving into a position beside him, Emily saw the way he was holding onto the banister for support. "You really should be back in bed," she insisted, afraid he was going to lose his balance and fall down the stairs.

Vivian showed no signs of being concerned about the seriousness of Jed's condition. "I brought a couple of gifts I'd like to give to the girls," she continued. As if the thought had just struck her, she gave a little shrug and said, "I never know what to get the boys. I'll leave a few dollars and you can get them something."

The children had gathered at the top of the stairs. "Girls, your grandmother has something for you," Jed said. "Go down and thank her."

Emily moved aside to make a path for Linda and Amy. As they passed their uncle they glanced up at him as if asking whether they really had to do this. He gave a little nod and they went on down.

"You two need some dresses," Vivian said, with a small reprimanding shake of her head as her gaze traveled over the shorts and T-shirts they were wearing.

Watching the trio, Emily sensed a coldness about the older woman even as she gave each girl a hug and handed them their gifts.

"Dolls," Drew muttered with disgust as the girls opened their packages and took out the beautifully dressed, delicate porcelain-faced figures. But Emily saw the hurt in his eyes.

"You must be careful with them," Vivian was cautioning the girls, touching the face of Linda's doll with a caress that was much more loving than any she had thus displayed toward her grandchildren. "You should find a safe place and keep them there to look at."

Linda glanced dubiously at Amy who was holding her doll precariously by the leg.

"Amy, dear, you really must be gentle," Vivian reprimanded. Taking the doll from the child, she handed it to Linda. "I will count on you to see that Amy doesn't break hers."

"I'll try," Linda replied as Amy stood looking puzzled, uncertain of what she had done to have her present taken from her.

Vivian gave the girls another hug. "And you must come and visit me one day," she encouraged, her attention focused only on them. Then, dropping a ten-dollar bill on the hall table, she left, with only a brief goodbye flung in the direction of the stairs.

"I'll never understand that woman," Thelma said from the dining-room door.

Jed didn't respond. Instead, he started to turn to go back to his room. But halfway round, he stopped and his hand tightened on the banister. "I could use a shoulder to lean on, Emily," he said.

Terrified he might fall, she quickly slipped under his arm and helped him back to his room. As they entered, the memory of their morning encounter assailed her and, again, embarrassment tinted her cheeks. But he had a distant look in his eyes and she had the feeling that he didn't even realize she was there. She could have been an inanimate object for all he cared. Good, she told herself.

"Thanks," he muttered as he stretched out on the bed, keeping his jeans on. The girls had come back upstairs and joined their brothers. "I left the dolls on the hall table," Linda informed Emily. "Could you find a safe place for them?"

She looked almost frightened to touch them. "I'll take care of them," Emily promised.

"Don't know how my sister-in-law grew up to be so nice with Vivian for a mother," Jed muttered.

"If I remember correctly, she spent a lot of time with her grandmother on her father's side of the family," Thelma responded, coming at that moment to a halt in the doorway. Her gaze shifted to the children. "I've just baked some cookies and need a few tasters to tell me if they're any good. How about coming down to the kitchen and letting your uncle rest?"

All four responded with enthusiasm and hurried after the housekeeper.

"Emily..." Jed said as Emily started to follow.

Pausing in the doorway she turned back to face him. Now that they were alone, was he going to say something about their morning encounter? She had hoped he would forget about it. Her shoulders stiffened with pride.

As he began to recite a list of chores he wanted to be certain Hank was seeing to, Emily breathed a sigh of relief. Apparently he had forgotten their earlier confrontation, or at least, preferred to forget it had happened. "I'll make certain they are taken care of," she assured him in businesslike tones, again starting out the door.

"There is one more thing," he said.

When she turned back to face him, his expression was shuttered.

"I don't consider the women in my life as notches in my bedposts," he said levelly. "And you're giving me a great deal more credit for womanizing than I deserve."

He hadn't forgotten. Even worse, he was watching her as if he expected some response. The last thing she wanted was to discuss his love life. "Then I apologize," she replied, and escaped into the hall.

Chapter Eight

The doctor came that evening and ordered one more day of bed rest for Jed. "Everything looks normal," he informed Emily. "The dizziness he was having this morning seems to be disappearing and he claims his headache has improved. His vision is clear. Pupils are fine. But just to be on the safe side, I want him to stay down for one more day."

"Did you tell him that?" she questioned, already worried about how she was going to manage to make Jed follow this instruction.

"He said it was fine with him," Doc Wilson replied. He gave a puzzled smile. "Sort of surprised me."

"He's full of surprises," she replied, figuring Jed had merely agreed in order to get rid of the doctor but had no intention of following orders.

However, Jed did stay in his room that evening and rested the next day without argument. Emily avoided him for her part, leaving Thelma to minister to him. But toward midafternoon, she began to worry. It wasn't like Jed Sawyer to give in so easily. Maybe he wasn't as cured as he'd made the doctor think. He just didn't want anyone to know.

The children were outside playing. After asking Thelma to keep an eye on them, she went up to his room. The door was open and he was lying on the bed in his jeans and a shirt, looking as if he was sleeping. But when she started to leave, he opened his eyes.

"Did you want something, Emily?" he asked.

"I was just wondering how you were getting along," she replied, wishing she had stayed downstairs. But she had come with a purpose, she reminded herself. Moving toward the bed, she studied him closely. "You've behaved so well, I started to worry that maybe you were really feeling badly and didn't want anyone to guess how badly."

He smiled. "Thought I would prove to you that I could be amenable."

It was a crooked charming smile, which caused her legs to weaken. *Get out before you make a fool of yourself again!* she ordered herself. "As long as you're fine, I'll leave so you can rest," she said, backing toward the door.

A seriousness came over his features. "Wait a minute. There's something I want to talk to you about."

He'd probably decided that it was too uncomfortable having someone around who he knew was attracted to him but who he wasn't attracted to. She'd miss the children but maybe it was for the best. Or maybe, he was going to try to apologize for not being attracted to her. That would be worse.

"Privately," he added. "Would you mind closing the door?"

Might as well get it over with, whatever it was, she reasoned. With a facade of calm dignity she did as she was asked.

Rising from the bed, he stood facing her. "This accident has caused me to take a closer look at my current situation. It has occurred to me that if something should happen to me, the children would have only Vivian to go to. I want to ensure a better future for them than that." His gaze narrowed on her. "Will you marry me, Emily?"

She stared at him in disbelief. "That blow to your head must have done more damage than we thought."

His scowl deepened. "This isn't a joking matter, Emily. I'm serious. Is that your way of saying no?"

She wetted her suddenly dry lips. She knew she should say no. Every instinct warned her that she would only be setting herself up to get hurt if she accepted. Still, a part of her wanted to say yes. "I just don't think it would work," she heard herself saying shakily instead.

"You've admitted to being attracted to me and I find you agreeably appealing. But even more important, the children are very attached to you and you seem to be attached to them." He paused as if waiting for a response to this last assumption.

"I do care for them a great deal," she admitted.

"And if they had their choice of an aunt, it would be you," he continued in a reasoning voice.

Pride caused her back to stiffen. "But I don't think that's a good reason for you to choose me."

He paced across the room, then came back to stand in front of her again, his jaw set in a determined line.

"You've been a surprise to me. You're a warm loving woman. I've seen it in the way you handle the children. And—" he smiled sheepishly "—in the way you've put up with me the past couple of days." His expression again became serious. "I trust you to raise the children with love and understanding."

Emily had always been practical, and that side of her told her this could never work. But the thought of being married to Jed filled her with a tantalizing excitement. Like the feeling a child gets just before they get on their first amusement park ride, she mused. Only this ride could prove to be a great deal more dangerous. A sudden thought caused a cold chill. "And while I'm raising the children, what will you be doing?" she asked.

He continued to regard her grimly. "I'll be raising them with you. I am a man of my word. When I make a vow, I keep it."

She knew her limitations. Just the thought of his having an extramarital affair caused her stomach to knot and she hadn't even agreed to marry him. "There are a lot of vows involved in a marriage ceremony," she pointed out.

"I intend to keep all of them."

He was promising her fidelity. But he didn't love her. He was only doing this for the children. It would never last, her practical side insisted. And there was one other matter that needed addressing. Watching him closely, she said, "Just in case you've forgotten, I cannot give you children of your own."

He gave a small shrug. "Four children is enough for any man to raise."

She wanted to marry him. She knew it would probably be the most stupid thing she had ever done or would ever do, but she wanted to do it more than she had ever wanted to do anything. "I would want your word that if you ever wanted out of the marriage, you would simply ask. You wouldn't have an affair behind my back or spend your life regretting never having a child of your own."

"You have my word," he replied gruffly.

This was crazy, her inner voice warned. But she wasn't listening. Pride refused to allow her to let him guess how much she wanted to marry him. "I'm not so certain it's the smartest thing either of us will ever do," she said levelly, "but it's the best offer I've had."

He regarded her dryly. "Can I assume that's a yes?"

The final *yes* stuck in Emily's throat. There was one more thing she had to do. "There's something you should see." Her cheeks reddened with embarrassment and she had to fight to keep her hands from shaking as she reached for the fastening of her jeans.

Jed cocked an eyebrow but said nothing as she popped the snap and unzipped the zipper.

With one hand, Emily lifted her shirt to just below her bra. With the other, she shoved the front of her jeans and underpants down far enough to expose the major portion of the scarring on her abdomen. Taking a deep breath, she forced herself to look at Jed.

"It must have hurt," he said, his gaze traveling over the newly exposed area of her body.

Her jaw tensed. "I'm not looking for your pity. I thought you should see what you would have to live with before we finalized anything."

He lifted his gaze to her face. "I was offering sympathy, not pity. There's a difference." His gaze traveled downward to the exposed area once again. Taking a step toward her, he ran his hand over the scars.

His touch left a trail of fire. Her stomach muscles tightened as a wave of poignant pleasure swept over her. She'd never felt anything so intense or so enjoyable.

Again he shifted his gaze to her face as his touch became firmer. Very slowly, he ran the palm of his hand over her rib cage. With his thumb he traced the bottom curves of her breasts and the pulse in her neck began to throb wildly. She'd never known a man's touch could be so stimulating.

The green of his eyes darkened and her breathing became more shallow as she was drawn into their jade depths. His hand moved lower over her hip. Down deep inside of her a fire began to burn. With the tips of his fingers he followed the line created by her lowered jeans and panties. As he let his fingers travel just under the barrier created by the clothing, teasing her with the hint of further intimacy, she thought that if she were a cat she would be purring.

Smiling with satisfaction, he kissed her lightly, then straightened away from her. "The scars won't bother me," he assured her, deftly pulling her clothing back into place and fastening her jeans.

Her heart was pounding a mile a minute. She hadn't wanted him to stop. It suddenly bothered her that she could be so strongly affected and he could so easily step away from her.

"If you don't stop looking at me that way, our wedding night's going to be a replay," he warned huskily.

Emily flushed with pleasure as she realized he hadn't been as unaffected by her as she had thought.

His manner became businesslike. "I'd like to go ahead with the wedding as soon as possible. If we apply for the license tomorrow we can pick it up on Monday. I can call Reverend Manord and see what time he'll be available on Monday. He can marry us either in his office or here." He paused. "Of course, if you'd rather have a more traditional wedding, we can wait a couple of weeks."

If she had time to think about it, reason might win and she'd back out. Besides there were the gossips to consider. "As soon as people hear we're going to get married, they'll think we're already sleeping together unless I move out of your house," she said matter-of-factly. "And I can't do that for any length of time because of the kids." Hoping to appear to be as nonchalant about this as he was, she gave a little shrug. "Monday's fine with me."

"Good," he said as if completing a deal. Smiling, he returned to the bed and picked up the phone. "As soon as I check with the Reverend, we'll go tell Thelma and the kids."

Emily was a little worried that, although the children liked her, they might see her as a threat to their uncle's affections. But they greeted the news with delight—even relief.

"Now you'll never leave us," Linda said, giving Emily a big hug.

Emily wished she could be so certain they would all remain together as a family. But whatever happened, she would see that the children stayed together.

Thelma accepted the news with a pleased I-told-you-so grin.

Even Reverend Manord accepted the marriage without the strong reservations Emily expected him to have. He was an elderly man who had served their community as its spiritual leader and adviser for nearly forty years. "I've married hundreds of couples," he said that evening as he sat in the living room with Jed and Emily after finalizing the details for the wedding. "More folks than I care to remember have come down my aisle more than once with different partners on their arms." He shook his head as if this bothered him greatly. "I suppose I should be counseling the two of you to proceed with caution. But—" he looked Jed straight in the eye "—I know Emily will make you a good wife and she'll be a good mother to those children. I expect you to be an equally good father and husband."

Emily had to fight to keep from smiling at the Reverend's manner. He was the only man she knew who would dare speak to Jed that way.

"I intend to," Jed replied solemnly.

The Reverend nodded with satisfaction. "Then you two have my blessing."

But later that night as she lay sleeplessly in her bed, Emily couldn't help wondering if she was doing the right thing. She hadn't been very successful at controlling her emotions where Jed was concerned. The attraction she felt for him was incredibly strong. "He's determined to find a mother for the children," she muttered, "so it might as well be me." But down deep inside she was certain that eventually he would grow tired of her and want his freedom. "By then I'll be tired of him, too," she assured herself.

By Saturday all the plans for the wedding were set. The guest list was small, only a few friends and of course Thelma and the children. It was to take place in the living room of Jed's house at two o'clock Monday afternoon. Cake and punch would be served afterward.

Emily had driven into Kansas City on Friday to find a dress. Since it wasn't to be a formal wedding, she'd found a simple white linen suit. She'd also bought herself a couple of sexy nightgowns.

Standing in the hallway Saturday night watching Jed playing with the children in the living room, she wondered if he would care what she wore. He was marrying her to provide security for the children. He'd already called his lawyer and arranged to have his will changed and to name her as their legal guardian in the event anything happened to him. Physically she would be just a warm body to satisfy his baser needs. And my own, she admitted in a surge of honesty.

The ringing of the phone startled her and she jumped. Picking it up on the second ring, she frowned. It was Howard.

"I can't believe you're going to marry Jed Sawyer," he said in hushed tones, causing her to guess he was calling from his home.

Her frown deepened. "And I can't believe you're calling me."

"You know I can't leave Mary now," he continued. "But you and I belong together."

"You belong with your wife and children," she replied, dropping the receiver into the cradle. As she stared at the phone another truth about Howard suddenly came clear to her. He had only asked her to marry him the first time after Jimmy Gyles had begun to show an interest in her. After the accident when he figured no one would want her, he deserted her. It wasn't until Jed Sawyer had come into her life that Howard had again shown an interest. "He's nothing more than a selfish spoiled child who only wants a toy when other people want it," she muttered under her breath, again grateful that she had never married him.

"Something wrong?"

Jerking around, she discovered Jed watching her from the doorway of the living room. "Nothing," she assured him.

For a moment he didn't look convinced, then he nodded and went back inside.

Sunday was more difficult than Emily had expected. News of her and Jed's impending marriage was already widespread.

"I'm so happy for you, dear," old Mrs. Jacobs said, catching Emily as, with Amy in tow, Emily was making her way toward the two- to four-year-olds' room. Lowering her voice, she added, "And I'm sure your mother will be resting much more easily in her grave. I didn't want to say anything before because I knew the children needed you, but I'm sure Joan would never have approved of your living under a single man's roof."

"We were well chaperoned by Thelma and the children," Emily replied stiffly.

Mrs. Jacobs gave her a quick little smile. "I know, dear," she said in a patronizing tone that suggested she didn't think Emily had been chaperoned at all. "But it's just so much better this way." Giving Emily a motherly pat on the hand, she continued on her way.

"I'm so embarrassed about last week," Cheryl Avery said when Emily joined her in the Sunday-school room. "I suppose you and Jed had a fight and that was why he asked me out. And there I was talking to you about whether I should date him or not."

"He's only marrying her for the children's sake," a female voice said bluntly from the doorway.

Turning, Emily saw Karen standing there.

"Jed's been so devastated by his brother's death, he's willing to do anything for those children," the redhead continued. Looking down her nose, she added with a hint of distaste, "Even marry Emily."

Emily met Karen's maliciousness with a cool silence. What the woman said was true and she thought she had accepted it. But the redhead's words caused a sharp bitter pain.

"You're just jealous because he was never willing to marry you," Cheryl said, coming to Emily's defense.

Karen smiled acidly. "As far as I'm concerned Emily is welcome to him and his brood." Her gaze swung across the room to where Amy was playing, and a look of pure disgust came to her face. "That one ruined my best dress." As her gaze swung back to Emily, she added with honey-coated sympathy, "And I suppose this is the only way you'll ever have a family to raise. I wish you the best of luck. You'll need it. Jed's never been the settling-down type." With a toss of her head, she turned and strode down the hall, her high heels clicking on the tiled floor.

"Don't let anything Karen says bother you," Cheryl advised in soothing tones. But in spite of the encouraging smile on her face, there was a worried look in her eyes.

Emily knew that deep down Cheryl agreed with Karen's assessment of the marriage. The painful truth was that it was an accurate picture. *You're crazy to go through with this,* she warned herself again. But again, she refused to heed the warning. Just this once she would do something foolish because she couldn't resist the temptation.

Monday arrived and Emily was a nervous wreck. As she and Jed stood in front of the Reverend exchanging their vows, it occurred to her that Jed had never even kissed her. The kiss to seal their wedding vows would be their first. That had to be some kind of record in this country in this day and age, she thought trying not to give in to the panic spreading through her.

Too late to bolt now, she told herself as the Reverend pronounced them husband and wife. Then Jed was kissing her. His lips were warm and enticing, and the strong feel of his arms around her sent a rush of excitement through her that vanquished her panic. *As long as I consider this marriage as a day-to-day arrangement with the probability of it ending at some point in the future, I'll be fine,* she assured herself.

But later that night as she showered and dressed for bed in one of her new negligees, renewed panic taunted her. All afternoon she had warned herself that this night might be a disappointment. She had no real idea of what kind of lover Jed was. He could be perfunctory, thinking only of himself. *You really did enter this like a blind fool,* she scolded the image in the mirror. *You let your hormones do your thinking for you. But even if Jed and I don't have a satisfying relationship, I will still have the children to love,* she argued philosophically. Taking a deep breath, she entered the bedroom.

"You do look tasty," Jed said, moving toward her. He was still dressed in his suit pants and shirt. Cupping her face in his hands, he kissed her lightly on the lips, then moved to her earlobe and nipped it gently.

Emily smiled as currents of pleasure shot through her.

His hand moved down to her neck. "You seem a little tense," he observed, an edge of coolness entering his voice.

"I'm just a little nervous," she admitted. "Actually I'm a lot nervous," she amended.

He frowned down at her. "I'm not going to attack you."

She hadn't meant to make him feel insulted. "I know," she replied, then heard herself confessing, "I'm a little worried about how I will compare to your other women friends."

The frown was replaced by a crooked smile. "I'll make you a deal—you don't compare me to anyone and I won't compare you."

She continued to regard him nervously. "I don't have anyone to compare you to."

Surprise registered on his face. "I figured you and Howard . . ." He let the sentence end itself.

Emily shook her head. "I'm the old-fashioned type."

A glimmer of mischievousness sparkled in his eyes. "Now I'm the one who's nervous. I'm going to have to do this right."

His teasing manner was infectious and she smiled back. "I was sort of counting on that."

Laughing lightly, he drew her into his arms. "We'll begin with a little necking," he said, and lowering his head began to nuzzle her neck.

"That tickles," she giggled, wiggling in his embrace. The movement brought her into closer contact, and as the heat of his body invaded hers currents of intoxicating pleasure surged through her.

"You're going to make taking this slowly very difficult," he warned, trailing kisses to the hollow behind her ear.

Her hands moved caressingly up over his shoulders. He felt so warm and inviting under her palms. "How slow do you think we should proceed?" she asked, rising up on tiptoe and kissing the hollow of his neck.

"Not too slow," he replied huskily, drawing her up more intimately against him. "I wouldn't want you to get bored."

"That would be terrible," she agreed as the feel of his firm body ignited primitive fires within her.

"Maybe we should move on to the shedding-our-clothes stage," he suggested.

Shocked by the intensity of the desire he had awakened, Emily had to fight to keep the impatience out of her voice. "That sounds reasonable." Her hands moved to the buttons of his shirt and she began to unfasten them. As the fourth button came loose and she began to work on the fifth, she couldn't resist the urge to kiss the newly exposed skin. The dark curly hairs of his chest felt rough but inviting against her lips, and she trailed kisses up to his neck as she finished with the unbuttoning.

"For an amateur, you're very good," he said huskily.

"I thought I should just let nature take its course," she murmured against his shoulder as she slipped the shirt off him.

"Sounds like a good method to me," he agreed, easing the robe of her negligee from her shoulders and letting it fall to the floor.

His touch felt like fire and her hands moved to the waist of his slacks.

A knock on the door suddenly interrupted. Drew's voice sounded from the other side. "Emily, Uncle Jed, Dennis says he has a stomachache."

Emily drew a shaky breath as a wave of frustration washed over her. "I'd better go check on him," she said regretfully.

"Yeah," Jed agreed, releasing her. Kissing her lightly, he added, "Just remember where we were."

"I will," she promised. Glancing down at the thin revealing robe on the floor, she added, "I think my old robe would be more appropriate." Going to the closet, she pulled out the functional terry-cloth garment.

In Dennis's room she found him sitting on the edge of his bed holding on to his stomach.

"It was probably the third piece of wedding cake that did it," Drew said with adult authority. "I told him he shouldn't have it."

Emily felt Dennis's forehead. He wasn't running a fever and three pieces of wedding cake could very easily explain his current discomfort. "I predict you'll live," she said gently. "I'll get you a little Alka-Seltzer."

Dennis forced a smile.

A few minutes later she had him tucked back into bed.

She went back into her and Jed's bedroom and found Jed waiting for her. "How's Dennis?" he asked.

"He's fine," she assured him.

"Then I suppose we could get back to where we left off," he suggested, unfastening her robe and slipping it off her shoulders.

"That sounds like a good idea to me," she replied as her body once again flamed beneath his touch.

"Emily." Linda's voice called through the door. "Dennis and Drew woke Amy up and she can't get back to sleep. I offered to read her a story but she wants you."

"So do I," Jed muttered in Emily's ear. Then with a good-natured sigh, he straightened away from her. "But I guess Amy had better be taken care of first."

As Emily pulled on her robe a second time and left the room she found herself wishing Jed would show a little impatience. These interruptions were straining her nerves, but he seemed to be taking them in his stride. Taking a woman to bed is old hat to him, she reminded herself. Besides, it wasn't as if she was special to him. These thoughts didn't make her feel any better. Curtly, she shoved them from her mind.

She read two books to Amy before the child finally dozed off again. After making certain Linda was securely tucked in, too, Emily crossed the hall and checked on the boys. Both were sleeping peacefully.

Maybe now we won't be disturbed, she hoped as she returned to the bedroom. But this time it was empty. "He probably got bored and went down to the kitchen for a snack, or to the den to watch television," she muttered, disappointed that he wasn't as anxious to continue with their lovemaking as she was. "I suppose I should be glad he isn't lying in bed sleeping," she added, trying to look on the bright side.

"Sleeping is most definitely not what I have in mind," a male voice assured her.

Turning, she found Jed standing in the doorway with his shirt back on and buttoned.

Reaching her in two long strides, he lifted her into his arms. "While you were in with Amy, I had Thelma move up to your old room. She'll take care of the children. You and I are going someplace where we can have some privacy."

So the interruptions *had* annoyed him! Emily couldn't deny the pleasure this admission caused. At least he wasn't as disinterested as she had been beginning to think. She circled her arms around his neck for added support as he started toward the stairs. "Where are we going?"

"To your place," he informed her, descending the stairs and heading toward the door.

"Shouldn't I get dressed?" she asked feeling suddenly shy as he carried her outside in her nightgown and robe.

"You already have too many clothes on to suit me," he replied gruffly, continuing toward his truck.

She considered arguing. She'd always led a very conservative life-style, which didn't include driving around at night with practically no clothing on. But the protest died before it reached her tongue. It felt too good being in his arms like this.

When they reached the truck, she opened the door and he seated her inside. A large picnic basket was already there.

"Supplies to keep our energy up," he explained, climbing in on the driver's side.

Emily smiled as she fastened her seat belt. "You're a lot more fun than I thought you would be," she admitted.

Reaching over, he ran his hand from her knee to the top of her thigh. "And I plan to prove I can be even more fun."

Her sensitivity to his touch was overwhelming. Immediately desire was rekindled. "I'm sure you can."

He gave a satisfied laugh as his hand returned to the wheel.

When they reached the house, he carried her up to her room and set her down, then went back to the truck for the basket of food.

Emily quickly opened some windows for air and turned on the ceiling fan, then grabbed a fresh set of sheets from the closet. She was beginning to make the bed when Jed returned. Looking up as he walked into the room, she let her gaze travel from his slightly rumpled hair to his partly open shirt to his dress slacks and highly polished cowboy boots. Her heart began to pound faster. He looked so appealingly masculine... and he was her husband. *That probably won't be permanent,* her inner voice cautioned. *Don't ever start thinking of him as yours.* Determined to keep her perspective clear, she reminded herself that if it wasn't for the children he would never have given her a second glance. With a sharp pull she fitted the bottom sheet into place.

Jed's expression became shuttered. "You're looking very pensive all of a sudden," he observed, setting aside the basket and sitting down in a chair to pull off his boots.

"I was remembering an old saying that my grandmother used all of the time," she heard herself admitting as she tucked the top sheet in at the foot of the bed. Damn, she cursed mentally. This wasn't the time for soul-searching.

As he started to strip off his socks, he paused and looked questioningly at her when she didn't continue. "And what old saying was that?"

She could have kicked herself. She didn't want to ruin this night with serious thoughts. Giving a little shrug as if it didn't matter, she said with schooled casualness, "She used to say 'You've made your bed, now you must sleep in it.'"

He grinned rakishly as he rose and walked to the opposite side of the bed to help finish tucking in the sheet. "Sleeping wasn't what I had in mind."

Emily's stomach knotted. Was this marriage nothing more than a joke to him? "She wasn't speaking literally. It meant something like 'You've chosen your path, now you must follow it.'"

Jed's expression became serious. "I know what it meant." His gaze narrowed on her. "Is this your way of saying you're having second thoughts about our marriage? If so, all you have to do is say so. I won't hold you to it against your will. That wouldn't be good for either of us."

She looked at him and her blood began to race. What the future brought didn't matter. She wanted this time with him. "No," she replied firmly, moving around the bed toward him. "I'm not having second thoughts." Discarding her robe as she walked, she added, "I believe we had reached the shedding-our-clothes stage."

"I believe so," he agreed huskily, as she began unbuttoning his shirt.

His hands moved exploringly along the curves of her body, and the fires he so easily ignited flamed into life. She would worry about the future when it came. Right now all she wanted was to lose herself in his touch. Discarding his shirt, she kissed his shoulder as her hands sought the fastening of his slacks.

"You're not as shy as I thought you'd be," he said gruffly.

"I have an inquiring mind," she bantered, easing his slacks from his hips. "I've always been anxious to learn new things."

Kicking his slacks off, he began to slowly remove the gauzy nightgown she was wearing. His hands taunted and tantalized her body as they trailed over her hips and to her breasts. As he removed the last of her clothing, she went into his arms hungering for the full feel of him against her. She'd never experienced anything this exhilarating. He filled her senses and her mind. Everything but the two of them was forgotten.

"I can see we're going to be moving on to step three fast," he murmured.

"Step three," she agreed, barely able to think beyond the fires of passion he had awakened within her.

But as he eased her back on the bed and discarded the remainder of his clothing, a sudden fear brought a chill. The doctors had told her she would have a normal sex life, but they couldn't know for certain.

Leaning down, Jed kissed her scars, then looking into her face, he said, "You tell me if I start to hurt you."

She hadn't expected him to be so thoughtful, but then he'd been a lot of things she hadn't expected.

Playfully he began to kiss her, first on the lips, then worked his way down her body. She giggled when he reached her stomach, then gasped with excitement and pleasure as he moved to her legs. Desire burned, blocking out her fear.

"Jed," she breathed his name in a pleading voice.

He understood.

For a moment her body tensed at the newness of being possessed, then the strangeness was gone and all she wanted was to please him as much as he was pleasing her.

Sunlight was streaming in the window when Emily awoke the next morning. Lying quietly on her side, she watched Jed sleeping. Just thinking about his touch caused the fires of desire to ignite within her.

A smile tilted the corners of her mouth as she recalled their picnic between their bouts of lovemaking. "It's a good thing I brought this food," he'd teased her. "A man needs sustenance to keep up with you."

"Morning," Jed drawled lazily, breaking into her thoughts and bringing her back to the present. Turning on his side, he traced the line of her jaw as he kissed her lightly.

It felt so right being there with him. "Morning," she replied.

"Hey, Jed, you up there?" a man's voice called from outside.

Emily recognized the voice as belonging to Hank Johnson. Obviously he was here to do his morning chores.

Pulling on his slacks, Jed went to the window. "Morning, Hank," he called out.

"Emily throw you out already?" Hank yelled back with a raucous laugh.

"We came here to get some *privacy*," Jed responded.

Hank laughed again. "Wish the wife and I had a place we could go to get some privacy from the kids. See you later."

Turning back toward the bed, Jed frowned regret-fully. "Speaking of kids, I guess we should be getting back home."

"Yes," Emily agreed with a sigh. She wanted him to herself for a while longer but not only was that wanton, it wasn't fair to Thelma. "I think I've got something here I can wear." Tossing off the sheet she climbed out of bed.

But as she stood looking in her closet for a pair of old jeans, Jed came up behind her and drew her up against him. "I'm sure Thelma can take care of the kids for a little while longer," he said, kissing her on the back of her neck.

"I'm sure she can," she agreed, forgetting about clothing.

Chapter Nine

The summer had come and gone. It was late fall now and the smell of winter was in the air. Bundled in a heavy sweater, Emily sat in a porch chair, her feet propped up on the rail. Harrington lay beside the chair and she petted him lazily as she sipped coffee. It was early evening but the days were growing shorter now and the sun had nearly set.

There was a quiet smile on her face. From inside she heard the sound of the children's laughter mingled with Jed's and a warm contentment enclosed her like a blanket. "I never thought coming here would turn out so well," she confessed to Harrington.

She and Jed had been married for nearly five months now. A thoughtful look came to her face. Admittedly, there had been a few rough moments— like the night he'd taken the children for ice cream . . .

July had been smoldering hot as usual, and it had become routine for Jed, Emily, Thelma and the kids to drive to the local ice-cream parlor a few nights a week after dinner. But on this particular day, the children had behaved badly. Maybe it had been the oppressive heat. Whatever it was, they'd argued and spatted all day until Emily couldn't take any more. Finally she'd told them they were to go to bed directly after dinner.

But Jed hadn't known this and they were as good as gold when he came in. After dinner, he'd suggested they all go for ice cream. Emily started to tell him that she'd told the children they had to go to bed, but the words stuck in her throat. Instead, she'd pleaded a headache and stayed at home while he and Thelma and the kids went into town.

Left alone at the house, she'd paced angrily. He'd undermined her authority. "But he didn't know," she reminded herself curtly. She should have told him about her ultimatum. "And I would have if we weren't married," she admitted, an anxious look coming into her eyes. The problem was she liked being married to Jed. She liked it too much. She was afraid to say or do anything that might make him angry or make him think she was a shrew. "This isn't healthy," she warned herself. But she wasn't certain what to do.

Thelma had left the dishes to be washed later when the heat of the day had had time to dissipate. Too tense to do nothing, Emily ran water into the sink and began washing them. She had finished the dishes and the pots and pans and was standing on the front porch watching the final rays of the setting sun when Jed and the others returned. The children climbed out of the car with guilt written all over their faces. Jed and Thelma had reprimanding scowls on theirs.

Immediately Emily wanted to wrap her arms around the children like a mother hen protecting her brood.

"Why didn't you tell me you had told them they had to go to bed right after dinner?" Jed demanded, reaching the porch ahead of the others. "Linda and Drew had an attack of conscience—*after* they had eaten their ice cream," he said pointedly. As the children filed past him into the house, he added, "They confessed."

"I'll get these culprits to bed. You and Jed need to have a talk and get your signals straight," Thelma said, following the children.

Drew paused at the door and looked back at Emily woefully. "We're sorry," he apologized with honest remorse.

"It's all right," she replied, giving them an encouraging smile. "I should have said something to Jed. Go on in and have your baths."

"Yes, you should have said something to me," Jed agreed as Thelma and the children disappeared into the house. He scowled impatiently at her. "Why didn't you?"

Emily's nerves couldn't take any more. She was not naturally the submissive type and trying to be agreeable all the time was a strain. "For the same reason I don't say anything about how irritating it is to me that you never put the cap back on the toothpaste," she replied. Panic suddenly flooded through her when she realized what she had said. But it had to be voiced. She couldn't live her life like this.

The scowl on his face deepened. "I don't understand."

Afraid of the rejection she might see on his face, she turned away from him and, silhouetted against the night sky, let her gaze drift to the horizon. "I like this arrangement we have." Suddenly afraid he might guess that he was the main reason she liked it so much, she added, "I enjoy being a mother to the children and you're a very satisfying lover."

A crooked smile tilted one corner of his mouth. "Thanks." His frown returned. "Then what's wrong? Clearly there's something bothering you."

"I'm afraid of saying or doing anything that will make you regret having married me," she confessed stiffly. She forced herself to face him. "But being totally agreeable and submissive isn't natural for me."

The crooked smile returned. "I had noticed you were especially mellow these days." He traced the line of her jaw with the tips of his fingers. "I was sort of hoping it was because I was being such a good husband."

He was teasing her. She felt as if her whole life was on the line and he was making a joke of it. "This is serious," she snapped. Again afraid he might read too much from her face, she turned toward the horizon. "I can't go on like this."

The smile vanished. Turning her back toward him, he cupped her face in his hands and forced her to look at him. "I know and I don't want you to. I want you to be yourself," he said gruffly. "I never expected you to be perfect." The smile returned, "And I certainly never expected you to be docile and totally agreeable. I've seen you on your grumpy mornings."

There was no rejection in his eyes. Emily drew a shaky relieved breath and a smile played at the corners of her mouth. "I'm never grumpy," she said in a bantering tone. "I'm just a little out of sorts once in a while."

His smile broadened. Suddenly, a seriousness came over his face. "About this cap-on-the-toothpaste business—"

"I most certainly never expected *you* to be perfect," she interrupted with mock exasperation.

He laughed, a deep warm laugh that made her feel good all over. "I hope not. Because I'm not." Leaning down, he kissed the tip of her nose. "But I'll try to put the cap back on in the future."

And he had.

She should have relaxed after that encounter. He'd made it clear that she was free to be herself, but her anxiety had lingered and risen again to the surface on a Sunday in August.

Jed had gone over to Hank Johnson's place after supper to discuss how many extra hands he wanted for harvesting and when he wanted them. She'd expected him back in a couple of hours but it had been close to midnight when he'd finally gotten home. At ten o'clock she'd paced by the phone a couple of times, but pride refused to allow her to call Hank's place. Going out onto the porch, she sat down in a chair, propped her feet up and tried to pretend she didn't have a care in the world, but one of the muscles in her back kept threatening to twist into a knot.

"Hank probably had a few men over and they're sitting around telling one another tall tales," Thelma said, stepping out onto the porch. "Jed's probably lost track of the time. You know how men can talk when they get together."

Emily glanced up at the housekeeper. This was Thelma's way of telling her not to worry. "I know," she replied.

"Jed's not used to having anyone waiting up for him at home," Thelma added as if Jed's tardiness needed further explanation. "His pa never did, and I sure couldn't wait until all hours and get my work done the next day." A flush suddenly came to her cheeks as if she thought she might have said too much. "Guess, I'll be turning in. Good night."

"Night," Emily replied. As the housekeeper went back inside, Emily's hands balled into fists and she fought back the wave of nausea that threatened. Thelma's defense of Jed's tardiness only caused the suspicions she was trying not to feel to surface fully. Maybe he wasn't at Hank's at all. Maybe he had been feeling the need for variety in his female companionship and had sought out an old girlfriend.

You're supposed to trust your husband, she chided herself. But she and Jed didn't have a traditional marriage. Still, he'd given her his word.

She told herself that was good enough for her, but the muscle in her back twisted painfully as a scene from that morning at church came back to taunt her. She and Jed had been in the corridor downstairs walking Amy to her Sunday-school room when they heard Karen loudly lamenting about Brian Davies having to be out of town for the next week. As they passed the redhead, Emily was certain she saw Karen toss Jed an inviting glance. He'd acted as if he hadn't noticed anything. But Emily couldn't stop wondering if his indifference had been merely an act and he was with Karen right now.

Harrington was lying beside her chair. Reaching down she scratched the old dog's head. "I wish I didn't care so much," she confessed. But she did care a great deal. "There's no use denying it," she continued in the same quiet, reluctantly conceding tones. "I'm in love with him. And I'm so jealous worrying about him being with someone else that it's a wonder my skin isn't the same shade of green as his eyes." The thought of his eyes brought a hard knot to her stomach.

The grandfather clock in the entrance hall chimed once for the half hour. Eleven-thirty. Tomorrow was a working day; surely Hank and the other men needed to get to bed.

Jed always liked to get to bed by ten. This thought caused the knot in her stomach to tighten.

"He's a good man and he gave me his word," she said firmly as if saying the words aloud would make them more believable.

Harrington issued a low growl as if in total agreement.

"The trouble is he's a man," she muttered worriedly. "And he's used to his freedom and he's not in love with me." It suddenly occurred to her that Jed might think she was hovering too closely over him if he found her waiting on the porch. Besides, she had her pride. Drawing a breath, she started to rise. "And he shouldn't find me sitting here waiting as if I have nothing better to do than to worry about his whereabouts."

But she was barely to her feet when Jed's truck turned into the drive. Even if she made a run for the door, he was certain to see her. "Caught," she muttered unhappily. "Might as well wait now."

"Sorry I'm late," he apologized, climbing out of the cab and slamming the door closed. "Hank got involved showing me the Studebaker he's been working on. It's a real classic."

"Is it late?" she asked with feigned surprise. "I guess I was enjoying the sunset and the peace and quiet so much that I forgot all about the time."

Joining her on the porch, he studied her. "I thought maybe you were waiting up for me."

The words to deny this formed on her tongue. But lies between her and Jed had only caused trouble. Besides, she needed to know the truth. She met his gaze fully. "I was," she confessed. Swallowing the lump trying to form in her throat, she added bluntly, "I thought maybe you had gotten bored with my company and found someone else to dally with for a while."

He frowned impatiently. "I gave you my word, Emily."

"I know." Now he was angry with her for not trusting him. The knot in her stomach tightened until it hurt. "But under the circumstances—you marrying me for the sake of the children and not because you really wanted to—it's only natural for me to wonder a little," she said in her defense.

He regarded her levelly. "We might not have married for conventional reasons, but I'm enjoying our marriage." His mouth suddenly tilted in a quirky smile. Placing a finger under her chin, he kissed her lightly. "And you give me a great deal more credit for stamina than I deserve. Keeping you satisfied is plenty for me."

Emily flushed. She had enjoyed his company in bed but she hadn't thought she had been that wanton. "I didn't think I was all that demanding."

His smile broadened. "I'm not complaining," he assured her. Drawing her into his arms, his hands moved down her back to the rounded firmness of her seat. "I'm not complaining at all."

She saw the desire in his eyes and a rush of womanly satisfaction swept through her. "I suppose we should be going inside," she suggested, kissing his neck then moving to the line of his jaw. She loved the taste of his skin.

"Sounds like a good idea to me," he conceded with a deep laugh. Keeping one arm around her, he turned her toward the door and guided her inside.

Emily's pulse quickened. Just thinking about Jed's touch could turn her body to fire. But it was his admission that he was enjoying being married to her that had meant the most to her. It was a memory she cherished because it gave her hope that their marriage would last.

They had even survived their first argument. Well, actually it hadn't been an argument. It had been more of a snit fit on Emily's part.

Thelma's sister had come down with a case of summer pneumonia just before harvest time, and Thelma had needed to go take care of her. That had left Emily with all the usual chores plus feeding the men who came to work. She hadn't minded. She'd been used to hard work all her life. But it had meant long days and falling into bed dead tired at night. When the harvest was over she had expected life to slow down a bit, but Jed decided he needed a new corral and shelter shed for some of his cows before the winter weather arrived. This required working extra hours. He was so exhausted when he came in at night he was asleep by the time his head hit the pillow.

Emily began feeling neglected, but she understood and told herself not to think selfishly. Then the children started coming down with the flu that was going around. It was only a forty-eight hour variety but they came down with it one after the other, and Emily was kept busy day and night for a week nursing them and didn't get much rest. By the time Thelma returned, Emily was worn out. But even more, she and Jed had barely had time to say a word to one another and she was feeling extremely neglected.

At noon on the day of Thelma's return, Jed asked Emily to run into town and pick up a part for a piece of equipment that needed repairing.

"Sure, no problem," she snapped. "That's all I'm good for around here anyway—to run errands, take care of the children, do the laundry, cook and clean!" Jed had looked shocked by her outburst. Before he had time to respond, she stormed into the kitchen, asked Thelma to watch the kids for a couple of hours and slammed out the back door.

By the time she reached the end of the driveway, hot tears were burning at the back of her eyes. She felt like a fool! She should never have snapped at Jed that way. He'd been working hard, too, and it wasn't unreasonable for him to ask her to run this errand. Normally she enjoyed doing things for him.

By the time she returned, she was almost too embarrassed to face him. But she knew she should apologize. Stopping by the house first, she went in to check on Thelma and the children before she headed out to the barn.

But as she entered the house, Jed came out of the living room. "I appreciate your going to get that piece of equipment for me," he said, his expression guarded as if he wasn't certain what to expect from her.

A pink flush tinted her cheeks. "I shouldn't have lost my temper the way I did. I didn't mind running the errand."

"Guess maybe we've both been working a little too hard lately." Approaching her, he traced the line of her jaw with the tips of his fingers. "I've missed having private time with you."

Emily's knees turned to jelly. She had absolutely no immunity to him at all. "I've missed it, too."

His guardedness disappeared and he smiled. "I'm glad to hear that. I've arranged with Thelma to take care of the children. I thought you and I could take a picnic dinner and go over to your place for the evening. We could spend some of that quality time together the marriage counselors on the television talk shows are always recommending for couples."

He was looking at her in a way that made her want to melt into his arms. "Some quality time sounds like a nice idea."

"The basket is packed and in the truck and I've got the situation here under control. You two get along," Thelma ordered from the door of the den.

"We're on our way," Jed replied, slipping an arm around Emily's waist and guiding her toward the door. A few minutes later as they drove toward her place, he reached over and playfully caressed her leg. "I have to admit, I've been feeling a little neglected with you spending more time lately in the children's rooms at night than in my bed."

"I didn't think you missed me," she heard herself admitting. "You've been working so hard you haven't even been able to keep your eyes open at night."

His expression became serious. "I've gotten real used to having you close by. I might not always be as attentive as I should be but I always know when you're not there."

Emily studied him covertly. Was he learning to care for her? Or was she just becoming a comfortable habit? Afraid to hope for too much, she decided she was probably a comfortable habit. But that was a start and some day she might be much more.

Some day. The words echoed in her mind as she returned to the present.

Jed's voice broke into her thoughts. "I'm getting ready to put the kids to bed. You want to say goodnight to them?"

"Yeah, I'm coming in," she replied.

There was a decided chill in the air now, and Harrington followed her inside and curled up on his blanket near the fireplace in the den.

In a few minutes Jed and Emily had the children tucked in for the night.

"I could use one of your massages," he said as they returned to the living room. "Must have pulled a muscle in my right shoulder. Hurts like the dickens."

Standing behind the couch, she began to work the knot out of the muscle. The fire in the fireplace had been banked for the night and the room was cooling, but she didn't notice. Just being with Jed made her happy and the feel of his hard body beneath her hands warmed her.

"I swear no one has your touch," he said as the muscle relaxed.

The peacefulness she had been feeling was suddenly shattered as she found herself picturing first Karen and then Josephine standing just as she was, massaging his shoulder. Who had stood there before didn't matter, she told herself. As long as he wasn't wishing she was someone else, she was satisfied. But she couldn't stop her insecurities from surfacing. Even after five months they were so very close to the surface.

Capturing her hand, he carried it to his lips and kissed it. "Come around here and sit by me," he requested.

Emily forced a smile. She had promised herself a zillion times she would consider this marriage a day-to-day arrangement, but she could not stop herself from hoping it would last a lifetime. She walked around the couch and sat down beside him.

"I have something for you," he said, opening the drawer of the table beside the couch and taking out a small prettily wrapped package.

Her smile became genuine. "A gift? What for?"

"For being you," he replied, kissing her on the tip of the nose as he handed it to her. His voice became a gentle caress. "The other day I was remembering how crazy I thought Thelma was when she suggested I ask you to come here and take care of the children. Now I am eternally grateful to her. I suppose I'm going to have to listen to her tell me 'I told you so' for the rest of my life, but it's worth it."

Emily's heart was pounding furiously and her hands shook as she opened the package. He was talking as if he expected this marriage to last a lifetime. Inside was a jeweler's box. Opening it, she found a ring—a diamond solitaire in a simple gold setting. It wasn't huge or fancy, but to her it was the most beautiful ring in the world—because it had come from Jed.

"We got married so quickly I never gave you an engagement ring," he was saying with a crooked smile. "I know this is a little backward, but I wanted you to have one."

"It's beautiful," she managed around the lump in her throat.

He took it out of the box and slipped it on her finger. A mischievous gleam sparkled in his eyes. "You've been like the surprise Christmas present under the tree—the one a person can never guess what's inside and they're worried it might be something they won't like or want. Then it turns out to be the best present of all."

Joy swelled inside Emily. "I like being the best present," she said, kissing him softly on the lips.

Laughing quietly, he stretched out on the couch, lifting her with him until they were both snuggled closely together. "And the best part is playing with you," he said, nibbling on her earlobe.

His hand moved possessively along the curves of her body, and Emily thought she might burst into flame at any moment. "Ah," she bantered. "The truth is out, you chauvinist. You consider me nothing more than a mere plaything."

"There is nothing *mere* about you," he returned, nuzzling her neck.

Emily curled her fingers in his hair. "You've worked out pretty good as a husband, too," she admitted.

Jed's head came up so he could look down into her face. "Only pretty good?" he demanded as his hand eased up under her sweater, spreading a trail of fire.

"Very good," she amended huskily.

"Uncle Jed, would you get me a glass of water?" a young voice suddenly asked.

Looking over Jed's shoulder, Emily saw Dennis standing in the doorway of the living room.

Jed groaned and freed her. "Sure thing, little guy," he replied.

Remaining on the couch as the two males headed toward the kitchen, Emily wrapped her arms around herself to hold on to the feelings filling her. Jed had been talking to her as if he cared—as if they were in love not just . . . in lust.

A couple of minutes later she heard him taking Dennis upstairs. As he came back down she snuggled against the back of the couch to give him room. But he didn't lie back down. Instead, he offered her his hand to help her to her feet. Obviously the moment of being playful lovers had passed, she decided regretfully, accepting his offer and rising. Suddenly she was being tossed over his shoulder. "I think it's time we moved this conversation upstairs where we can lock our door and have some privacy," he said, starting toward the stairs.

Again excitement and happiness welled within her. "I would have walked," she said with mock indignation.

He ran his free hand along the back of her leg. "My mother used to always make me carry my toys upstairs."

Laughing softly, she submitted without any further protest.

Chapter Ten

"Think I hear a car coming up the drive," Thelma said, looking up from the cookie batter she was spooning onto the baking sheet.

It was a Wednesday in early December. The three older children were in school and Amy was upstairs having her afternoon nap. Emily and Thelma were baking cookies in preparation for the coming holidays and Jed was out by the barn repairing a fence.

"Probably someone to see Jed," Emily replied, carefully wrapping a finished and cooled batch of butter cookies to be put in the freezer.

Thelma was straightening from having placed a fresh batch of cookies in the oven to bake when a knock sounded on the front door. "I'll see who it is."

Returning to the kitchen a couple of minutes later, she had a look of disapproval on her face. "You've got a visitor."

"Who?" Emily asked, wondering who would have caused the housekeeper to look so disagreeable.

"Howard Parker," Thelma announced with distaste. "He said he had to talk to you. He's in the living room."

Emily couldn't believe Howard had the nerve to come to her home, especially after the prank he pulled that could have cost Jed his life. "I'll get rid of him," she muttered, forgetting about the cookies and heading toward the door.

"Afternoon, Emily," Howard greeted her as she entered the living room.

"What are you doing here?" she demanded, then as a second thought added curtly, "Never mind. I don't want to know. I just want you to leave."

His manner became contrite. "I need to talk to you, Emmy."

She shook her head. "We have nothing to talk about."

His face screwed into a little-boy pout. "Everyone's talking about how happy Jed seems to be. It should be me. I know it's my fault you and I aren't together, but we can change that."

Emily glared at him. "In the first place, I'm not interested in changing anything. In the second place, I can't believe you came here after your little prank last summer got Jed hurt."

Howard's expression became even more boyishly pleading. Moving toward her, he captured her hand. "I know you're angry with me. You have every right to be. I should be boiled in oil for the way I treated you. But I'm begging for your forgiveness."

"Go home," she ordered attempting to free her hand.

His hold on her tightened. "That's just the point, Emmy. I haven't got a home. I've decided to leave Mary. It's you and I who should be together. It's me you should be making happy, not Jed Sawyer."

Emily stared at him with disgust. "You're nothing more than a spoiled child," she said, seething. "When you thought no one would be interested in me, you dropped me like a hot potato. Now that I've got a husband and he's happy with me, you want me back."

"What's going on here?"

Emily jerked her hand free as Jed strode into the room. "Howard was just leaving," she said coolly.

A malicious gleam sparked in Howard's eyes, but as he turned to Jed, his expression held only regret. "First, I want to apologize for that little prank we pulled so that we could have some undisturbed time together. If we'd known that Jeep would throw you, we'd never have done it."

Emily's face flushed crimson with fury. Howard had made it sound as if she had been a partner to his plan. "It wasn't—" she started to explain hotly that she had not been a participant.

Jed cut her short. "So it was you who called about the bull," he growled, his jaw twitching with controlled anger as his gaze narrowed on Howard. Suddenly his attention swung to Emily and there was ice in his eyes. "No wonder you were so determined to nurse me back to health. You must have felt pretty guilty."

"I—" she started to explain again.

Howard glanced at her and the malicious gleam sparked in his eyes once again. Before she could say another word, he turned back to Jed. "I've decided to leave Mary," he interjected in a resolute voice that suggested this decision had come after much soul-searching. "I've realized that keeping our marriage together simply because of the children will only cause pain in the end." He turned back to Emily and the malicious spark came back into his eyes. "I came by to try to talk Emily into coming with me, but she's refused. She's very attached to your children. I've tried to convince her it's a mistake to stay. We belong together. But she feels her duty is here."

"That's—" Emily began.

Jed again cut her short. "Emily has no reason to feel duty bound to us." His manner became cool and indifferent. He gave a nonchalant shrug. "If she wants to leave that's fine with me."

All the protests died within Emily. She stood dumbly staring at Jed. He didn't care. She could walk through that door and never come back and he wouldn't care. She felt as if she had been kicked in the stomach.

As if he was suddenly bored with this conversation, Jed strode from the room.

"Guess you haven't been keeping him as satisfied as people think," Howard said. "Glad I found that out now before I actually broke with Mary."

"Get out!" Emily ordered, finding her voice.

"Yeah, I will," he replied, adding with a smile, "I've got a wife and kids to get back to."

Emily barely noticed Howard leaving. All she could see was the indifference on Jed's face. Bile rose in her throat. She had begun to think that he was learning to care for her. Her gaze dropped to the ring he had so recently given her. With a shaky hand, she pulled it off. Then she pulled off her wedding band.

The walls seemed to be closing in on her.

"You all right?" Thelma asked, entering the room. "You look pale as a ghost."

Emily blinked and forced herself to focus on the housekeeper. "I'm fine," she answered automatically. But she wasn't fine. Hot tears were burning behind her eyes and she felt nauseous.

Thelma frowned worriedly. "You don't look fine."

Emily's jaw tensed. She wanted to scream, do something to release the pain inside of her. But her pride refused to allow her to publicly display her hurt. She'd been a fool. "I need some time to myself," she heard herself saying, and she marveled at how calm she sounded.

The worry on Thelma's face deepened. "What did Howard want? What did he say?" Her mouth formed a hard line. "I knew I should never have let him in. He's always been a sneaky little troublemaker." She smiled encouragingly. "Whatever it was, don't you let it bother you."

"It wasn't anything Howard said or wanted," Emily replied. She started to say that it had been what Jed had said, but the words stuck in her throat. "I just need some time to myself," she said again and, brushing past the housekeeper, took the steps two at a time.

But as she entered the room she and Jed had shared, she began to tremble. With proud dignity, she walked over to his side of the bed and dropped her rings into the ashtray he used for the loose change from his pockets. The tears behind her eyes burned hotter. She had to get out of there.

She went back downstairs and found Thelma in the kitchen. "I'm sorry to desert you like this, but I have to have some time to think. I'm going over to my old place for a couple of days."

The housekeeper stared at her in surprise. "A couple of days?"

Emily nodded.

Thelma studied her anxiously. "I thought I heard Jed come in while Howard was here," she said coaxingly.

"He did," Emily replied stiffly. The expression of indifference on his face loomed in her mind. "I've got to go," she said and fled from the room.

Pulling on her coat as she strode out the front door, she headed for her car. A bark of welcome came from Harrington. Looking in the direction from which the bark had come, she saw the old dog seated on his haunches beside Jed. Jed was near the barn, standing by the corral fence he had been mending. He was watching her, but he made no move toward her.

Why would he? He didn't care what she did or where she went. She had thought she could handle it. She'd told herself a zillion times he wasn't in love with her. But she had begun to think he was, or at least learning to be. Damn! She cursed herself for letting a fantasy take hold of her mind. She whistled for Harrington. For a moment he hesitated, looking at Jed as if asking if he should go.

"Stay if you want," she muttered under her breath, climbing into her car.

But before she could close her door, Harrington trotted up. She got out, then opened the back door and let him in. She couldn't stop herself from looking back at Jed. He was still standing where she'd first seen him. Clearly he wasn't interested in even speaking to her and he sure wasn't going to make any move to stop her from leaving. *You didn't expect him to,* she chided herself. He'd been willing to believe the worst of her without even giving her a chance to defend herself. Slamming the back door, she climbed in behind the wheel.

The tears started about the time she reached the main road. They rolled down her cheeks like rivers. Angrily she brushed at them. "It's stupid to cry over a man who was never in love with you," she admonished herself. "He was always perfectly clear about our arrangement. I was the one who started living in a fantasy world."

She forced herself to concentrate on her driving, but in the back of her mind, Jed's image lingered. "Fool! Fool! Fool!" she screamed at herself.

Turning onto her property, she was glad she hadn't rented it or, even worse, sold it. Several people had approached her about one or the other, but she'd refused. This was her sanctuary, her place to go if the marriage didn't work out. Lately, however, she'd begun to think of Jed's place as her home, and she'd been seriously considering renting this place. "Good thing I didn't," she muttered.

"We're home," she announced to Harrington in firmer tones as she parked.

The house was chilly inside, but she barely noticed. It matched her mood. She went upstairs and made her bed. Her hands shook as images suddenly filled her mind. Since their wedding night, she and Jed had come here several times to have some privacy. Grudgingly she admitted that was another reason she had been so hesitant about renting. She liked having a place where they could get away together and she could have his undivided attention.

"You were such a fool to think he could really love you!" she snapped at her image in the mirror. Going back downstairs, her limp seemed suddenly more pronounced. For months now she hadn't even thought about it. Jed had made her feel so complete, so pretty. Tears threatened again.

Refusing to let them flow, she went out back. There was still a stack of firewood left from the previous winter. Carrying some inside, she started a fire in the fireplace in the living room. Oblivious to the fact that she was still wearing her coat, she sank into the overstuffed chair that had been her favorite and watched the flames take hold. For a long time she just sat there not thinking about anything, keeping her thoughts blocked and concentrating on the fire.

Outside, night came and the house grew dark except for the light cast by the flames.

"You hungry?" she asked Harrington at last. "I think there's a couple of frozen dinners in the freezer."

He looked up from where he was lying near the fire, then laid his head back down to show disinterest.

"I'm not hungry, either," she said, forcing herself to her feet, "but the fire is going to need more wood."

She carried in two more armloads. After feeding some of the wood to the fire, she again curled up in the chair. The room had warmed considerably, but still she kept her coat on. There was a coldness inside of her no amount of heat could vanquish. The images of the children came into her mind. The thought of giving them up tore her apart. If Jed agreed, she would still help with their care. But her marriage to him was over.

Her head was pounding. Closing her eyes, she dozed. The fire had nearly died when she awoke. A glance at her watch showed it was after eleven. "I suppose I should go to bed," she muttered. But she couldn't. Not yet. She and Jed had shared that bed. "Tomorrow I'll be strong enough to put him out of my mind, but not tonight," she admitted. Rising from the chair, she threw a couple more logs on the fire, then curled up once again.

"Tomorrow will be a better day," she assured herself as she dozed once again.

The sound of a knock on the front door woke her. Groggily she looked at her watch. It was two in the morning and the fire was dying once again. The sound of the door being opened and footsteps in the hall brought her to her feet. They stopped at the foot of the stairs.

"Emily." Jed called her name in cold clipped tones.

His voice made it clear he hadn't come to make peace. Just as well, she told herself. She couldn't go back to him. She knew now that he would never love her and she couldn't live as his wife with that reality. She, also, wasn't ready to face him. Standing frozen, she hoped he would go away.

"Emily!" he called her name a second time, this time more curtly.

The determination in his voice was uncompromising. He wasn't going to go away. Steeling herself, she said levelly, "I'm in here."

His steps moved toward the living room. She braced herself as he entered and switched on the light.

"Guess Howard's running a little late," he said, his gaze raking over her.

The cynical edge in his voice stung. Pride came to her rescue. "I'm not expecting Howard," she replied. Tired of being put on the defensive, she added dryly, "In fact, I wasn't expecting anyone to show up at this hour."

He cocked an eyebrow in disbelief. "You always sit around the living room in your coat?"

Glancing down at herself, she realized she was still wearing the heavy garment. "I was cold," she said with a forced nonchalant shrug. Seeing him was seriously threatening her control. *Don't do something stupid like cry in front of him,* she ordered herself as hot tears burned behind her eyes. Needing to avoid looking at him, she turned away and busied herself with putting a couple more logs on the fire. But the diversion didn't help. She could feel him watching her and she suddenly felt ugly and clumsy. She had to get rid of him. Straightening, she faced him. "Why are you here?"

"Thelma and the kids were worried about you. They wanted to know when you were coming back." His jaw hardened. "I want to know *if* you were coming back."

He sounded callous, as if her answer meant nothing to him. "No," she said tightly. "I'm not coming back."

"It's your decision," he replied coolly and strode out of the room.

Emily felt herself trembling. That was it. It was over. And he couldn't have cared less.

Abruptly his steps came to a halt. For a long moment the house was filled with a heavy silence. Then Jed strode back into the living room. "I always thought you were a reasonable sensible woman," he growled. "I can't believe you would throw your life away on a man like Howard Parker."

"I am not throwing my life away," she replied tightly.

"They say love is blind, but a woman would have to be totally senseless not to realize the guy's a jerk," he scoffed.

He actually thought she was in love with Howard. He had to think she was an idiot. "Let me put this as succinctly as I can," she said with cool dignity. "I am not in love with Howard and I have no intention of spending any part of my life with him."

He frowned in confusion. "Then I don't understand why you're here." He shifted uncomfortably. "If it's guilt because of my accident, you don't have to feel any. I turned the Jeep too fast. It was my own dumb fault."

Her jaw stiffened with anger. "It's not guilt. I had no part in the prank Howard played." Her jaw stiffened even more. "And I *never* planned any rendezvous with him. He merely gave that impression to cause trouble. He's a spoiled, selfish man. Even before the accident I was having my doubts about marrying him." She was talking too much. Suddenly afraid the hurt she was feeling might begin to show on her face, she turned away from him. "Please, just go away," she ordered.

But he made no move to leave. "You're not making any sense. If you're not in love with Howard and you're not planning to go away with him, why won't you come back to me and the kids? I thought you cared for them."

The hot tears welled in Emily's eyes. She wanted to go back but she couldn't. Jed didn't love her now and he never would. "I do care." She swallowed back the lump that threatened to form in her throat. "I was hoping we could work out some sort of arrangement. I could watch them during the day and maybe they could spend the night here with me once in a while."

"In other words, it's just me you want to cut out of your life," he clarified.

The tears burned hotter. "That's about it," she said. "Now will you please leave?"

Again a silence filled the room. Her hands balled into fists as she fought to maintain her control. A single tear rolled down her cheek. Damn! She couldn't cry in front of him. She wouldn't! Brushing away the thin stream of water, she turned and glared at him. "Get out!" she ordered through clenched teeth.

He stood watching her, his expression shuttered. "I thought we had a good thing going."

"I thought we did, too," she admitted. In her mind's eye she again saw him saying that it was fine with him if she left. Her control snapped. "Like a stupid fool, I thought you were even learning to care for me. But you made it clear today that..." Suddenly realizing what she was saying, humiliation brought a flush to her cheeks. Clamping her mouth shut, she turned away from him. "Get out!" she ordered again.

"I do care," he said gruffly.

She wanted to believe him. But she'd been enough of a fool already. "I was there, remember?" she snapped, jerking around to face him once again. "I heard you say it was fine with you if I left. I was free to do whatever I wanted to do." A deep bitterness swept through her. "What happened? Did it suddenly occur to you that you'd lost your baby-sitter...that you had the kids on your own again?" Hurt and humiliation mingled with the bitterness. That's all she'd ever been to him—just someone to help him raise the children. "I guess that caused you to have some serious second thoughts." Feeling another tear escaping, she jerked back around toward the fire.

"What occurred to me was that I was losing the woman I loved."

Emily froze in shocked disbelief. She was so upset she was hearing things, she told herself. She stood immobile, unable to turn to face him. She wanted to believe him but was afraid to.

"That was pride you heard talking this afternoon," he continued gruffly. "I'd figured all along you were still in love with Howard. After you recovered from the accident, you kept men at arm's length. I figured you had to have cared for him a lot for him to hurt you that badly. Then that Sunday when I found him here with you, that confirmed my belief."

Emily forced herself to face him. "It was distrust, not a broken heart that caused me to keep men at arm's length. I was humiliated by the way he treated me. I felt like a fool. I never wanted to be put in that position again." Her jaw tensed. "And it was Howard who sought me out. I didn't go looking for him."

He took a step toward her and a pleading quality entered his voice. "Emily, stay with me."

It took every ounce of her control not to run into his arms. But she couldn't make a mistake this time. "Are you sure it's love and not just panic at being left on your own with four children again?" she asked, feeling as if her whole life hung in the balance with his answer.

Reaching out, he touched her jaw caressingly. "Watching you leave today, I felt as if a part of me was being ripped out. Tonight I sat in my truck for four hours watching this place and trying to think of what I could say that would make you come back to me. I even considered bringing the children over here and using them. But I'd already used them once before." A look of embarrassment crossed his features. "After you moved into my home, I couldn't believe how attracted I was to you. I told myself it wasn't rational. I remember the first time I saw you in my kitchen late at night. You were in a light cotton nightgown and robe, barefoot and with your hair all mussed. I didn't think I'd ever seen a woman look so inviting. It started me thinking about you and me, but you insisted on keeping a distance between us." He shook his head. "And I tried, but the night you went out with Tom, I was ready to lock you in your room to keep you home."

"You had a date with Karen," she reminded him, still afraid to believe him.

"I thought she could take my mind off you, but it didn't work," he confessed. "If she hadn't left early on her own, I'd have sent her home."

Emily studied him dubiously. "What about Cheryl Avery?"

He grimaced. "I thought maybe dating her might give me some idea of how to approach you."

Emily stared at him, disbelief still strong in her eyes. "You asked me what I thought she would say if you asked her to marry you for the sake of the children."

"I was really asking you what you would say," he corrected. "But you avoided the answer. I figured you didn't want to have anything to do with me for any reason." He grinned crookedly. "Then I had the accident. That second day when you were undressing me to force me back to bed, as sick as I was feeling I was having trouble keeping my hands off you. Then I realized that the feeling was mutual. After you admitted that you were physically attracted to me, I couldn't stop myself from trying to persuade you to marry me, even if I knew you were only doing it for the children's sake."

He cupped her face in his hands. "I want you back, Emily. I'd like to believe that someday you could learn to love me, too. But it doesn't matter. I'll take you any way I can get you."

He actually looked desperate. "I do love you," she confessed as tears began to roll down her cheeks. "I left because I didn't think you cared, or would ever really care, for me."

Drawing her into his arms, he crushed her to him as if he was afraid she might suddenly slip away. "I've been half-crazy thinking I'd lost you." Leaning down, he feathered kisses over her face and hair. "Let's go home."

"Yes, let's go home," she agreed.

From near the fire, Harrington gave a sharp little bark to let them know he felt the same.

Emily awoke the next morning snuggled against Jed. The sun was high and she realized that she'd slept until nearly midmorning. But then it had been almost morning when they'd gotten home. Home. The word played through her mind. This was her home now.

Smiling, she remembered Thelma's greeting. The housekeeper had been sleeping in Emily's old room in case the children needed her during the night. She came into the hall when she heard Emily and Jed coming up the stairs. "I told him he was an idiot if he came back without you," she said with an approving nod when she saw that Emily was with Jed.

"We'll be sleeping in in the morning," Jed had informed her.

Thelma had smiled knowingly and gone back to bed.

Lazily, Emily ran her hand caressingly over Jed's chest. In her mind's eye she saw Mrs. Gyles saying, "I'm so glad you found a nice little niche for yourself."

It most certainly was a nice little niche, she conceded with a warm smile as she stretched, then lifted her head to place a light kiss on Jed's jaw. He loved her! Her smile broadened. He loved her! She wanted to laugh with joy.

Jed's arm along her back tightened possessively. "Morning," he said, turning to kiss her soundly.

"Morning," she replied against his lips.

"Been thinking I should get Thelma something extra-special for Christmas this year," he said. "I owe her a lot."

Emily breathed a satisfied sigh. "Me, too." From the hall she heard the patter of little feet and Linda calling out to the boys that Thelma was making cookies again. Two more sets of feet made a run for the stairs. Emily smiled softly, then a seriousness came over her features. "I want to thank you for giving me a family. I never thought I would ever be this happy."

"It's my pleasure," he replied. His hand moved leisurely along the lines of her body. "Believe me, it's my pleasure."

Emily giggled as he tickled her. Then his touch became seductive and her body flamed with desire. "The pleasure is mutual," she assured him.

* * * * *

**Star-crossed lovers?
Or a match made in heaven?**

Why are some heroes strong and
silent . . . and others charming
and cheerful? The answer is
WRITTEN IN THE STARS!

Coming each month in 1991,
Silhouette Romance presents
you with a special love story
written by one of your favorite
authors—highlighting the hero's
astrological sign! From January's
sensible Capricorn to December's
disarming Sagittarius, you'll
meet a dozen dazzling and
distinct heroes.

Twelve heavenly heroes . . . twelve
wonderful Silhouette Romances
destined to delight you. Look for
one WRITTEN IN THE STARS
title every month throughout
1991—only from Silhouette
Romance.   STAR

proudly presents
the long-awaited ''prequel'' volume of

★ LOVE AND GLORY ★

by
LINDSAY McKENNA

Dawn of Valor

In the summer of '89, Silhouette Special Edition premiered three
novels celebrating America's men and women in uniform: LOVE
AND GLORY, by bestselling author Lindsay McKenna. Featured
were the proud Trayherns, a military family as bold and patriotic
as the American flag—three siblings valiantly battling the threat
of dishonor, determined to triumph . . . in love and glory.

Now, discover the roots of the Trayhern brand of courage, as
parents Chase and Rachel relive their earliest heartstopping
experiences of survival and indomitable love, in

Dawn of Valor, Silhouette Special Edition #649.

This February, experience the thrill of LOVE AND GLORY—from
the very beginning!

DV-1

 *Silhouette Books*

Take 4 bestselling love stories FREE

Plus get a FREE surprise gift!

SILHOUETTE·INTIMATE·MOMENTS

NORA ROBERTS
Night Shadow

People all over the city of Urbana were asking, Who was that masked man?

Assistant district attorney Deborah O'Roarke was the first to learn his secret identity . . . and her life would never be the same.

The stories of the lives and loves of the O'Roarke sisters began in January 1991 with NIGHT SHIFT, Silhouette Intimate Moments #365. And if you want to know more about Deborah and the man behind the mask, look for NIGHT SHADOW, Silhouette Intimate Moments #373, available in March at your favorite retail outlet.

NITE-1

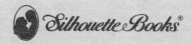

Silhouette Books®

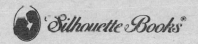

Silhouette romances are now available in stores at these convenient times each month.

Silhouette Desire **Silhouette Romance**	These two series will be in stores on the 4th of every month.
Silhouette Intimate Moments **Silhouette Special Edition**	New titles for these series will be in stores on the 16th of every month.

We hope this new schedule is convenient for you. With only two trips each month to your local bookseller, you will always be sure not to miss any of your favorite authors!

Happy reading!

Please note there may be slight variations in on-sale dates in your area due to differences in shipping and handling.